A
Harlequin
Romance

OTHER
Harlequin Romances
by RUTH CLEMENCE

Many of these titles are available at your local bookseller,
or through the Harlequin Reader Service.

For a free catalogue listing all available Harlequin Romances,
send your name and address to:

HARLEQUIN READER SERVICE,
M.P.O. Box 707, Niagara Falls, N.Y. 14302
Canadian address: Stratford, Ontario, Canada N5A 6W4

or use order coupon at back of books.

WIFE
MADE TO MEASURE

by

RUTH CLEMENCE

Harlequin Books

TORONTO • LONDON • NEW YORK • AMSTERDAM • SYDNEY • WINNIPEG

Original hardcover edition published in 1976
by Mills & Boon Limited

ISBN 0-373-01985-8

Harlequin edition published July 1976

Printed in U.S.A.

CHAPTER ONE

'WAKE up! It's turned eight.' Janey's melodious voice brought Jocelyn out of a pleasant dream. She sat up abruptly, still half asleep, to be brought wide awake by an indignant cry from her friend.

'What have you done to your lovely long hair?' she wailed as she collapsed on to the end of the bed, still wearing her night duty uniform and cloak.

Jocelyn squinted across at the mirror on the other side of the room in an attempt to have another look at her new short haircut. 'Does it look awful? I worked late last night with Simon arranging the reception for his mother and that cover girl she's bringing over from America for the charity show we're organizing. Carl dropped by to tell Simon about the refresher course he's been attending at his school of hairdressing and according to him, long hair is right out this season. He wanted a guinea-pig to show Simon his new ideas and I just happened to be the only female left in the building.'

'And I suppose it never occurred to you to say you liked your hair as it was? Surely your Carl could have demonstrated on a dummy?' Janey sounded thoroughly disgusted. 'Honestly, Jo! Why don't you stand up for yourself once in a while? Oh yes, I know,' she went on as Jocelyn opened her mouth to protest, 'Mrs. Wadebridge and your mother were old friends and she gave you your first job when she and Simon opened the agency, but that doesn't mean she and her high-and-mighty son own you body and soul. Why, you could get a job anywhere. Your brains and ability would be an asset to any office. Some high-powered executive would jump at the chance of getting his hands on you. Speaking metaphorically, of course,' she added with a twinkle in her eyes.

Janey Rushwick was never slow to speak her mind. She and Jocelyn had shared schooldays and since Janey passed her nursing exams, a small flat within easy walking distance of Janey's hospital.

'I daresay I could get another job,' Jocelyn replied thoughtfully, 'but it would seem a bit disloyal after all Simon and Mrs. Wadebridge have done for me.'

'Are you sure that's the only reason you put up with their extraordinary demands on your time and patience?' Janey asked.

Jocelyn's eyes opened wide in surprise. 'What other reason could there be?' she inquired innocently. 'Surely you don't think I stay for the perks?'

'If by perks you mean free make-up and a regular shampoo and set, no, I don't,' Janey's tone was tart. 'Nor do I mean all the clothes Mrs. Wadebridge buys for you. I was just wondering if under that cool, imperturbable exterior burned a secret yen for the great man himself?'

'Simon? You must be joking. No chance.' There was no mistaking the note of sincerity in Jocelyn's voice as she scrambled out of bed. 'Since our families were neighbours in the old days I've known Simon far too long to nurse a secret passion for him. As a matter of fact he scares me half to death. You ought to be at the office if anything goes wrong,' she finished as she headed for the bathroom, 'he's like a Force Ten gale in action.'

Jocelyn was washed and half dressed, making up her face, when Janey returned to the bedroom carrying a tray with two mugs of coffee and a plate of crisp buttered toast. As Janey put the tray down Jocelyn said, 'I've no time to eat. The buses are invariably full if I get to the stop after eight-thirty.'

'Nonsense!' Janey replied flatly. 'One of the first things we were taught as student nurses was never miss a meal. The agency won't grind to a halt if you're two minutes late, and I'd bet my last pound that Simon would be far from pleased if you fell in a faint in the middle of his office carpet from lack of food. In any case, think of all the unpaid overtime you do. You've not been home to have supper with me before I departed for night duty once all this week.'

'I know, and I'm sorry,' Jocelyn apologized, and to mollify her irate friend, bit into a finger of toast. 'We've been extra busy with Mrs. Wadebridge away,' she explained as she slipped a simple dress in a bitter chocolate shade over her head. She tied a cream scarf at the neck, stepped into matching court shoes and to take Janey's mind off Simon Wadebridge's autocratic demands asked, 'How do you like this dress? There's a jacket to go with it.'

She hoped the outfit really suited her, for free choice of her own wardrobe seldom came Jocelyn's way. Mrs. Wadebridge thought a neat uncluttered appearance a 'must' for her son's secretary and insisted on selecting Jocelyn's clothes. Repayment was always brushed aside, so Jocelyn had learned to submit with as good a grace as possible.

The morning's mail came cascading through the letter box just as she was about to set off for work. There were two letters for Janey, the electricity bill and one letter for Jocelyn herself, addressed, she saw with a sinking heart, in her younger brother's almost illegible scrawl.

Correspondence from him usually spelled trouble. Past experience warned her that the letter in her hand would certainly contain some plea for assistance. If she was to reach the agency by nine it must be read later, so she stuffed it into her handbag and calling out 'goodbye' to Janey, hurried off.

She was out of breath when eventually she pushed open the big plate glass door leading into Wadebridge's model agency, for four buses had passed her stop before there was room for Jocelyn to squeeze on. She stopped a moment just inside the door to inhale the mixture of perfume from the beauty salon and a subtle fragrance given out by the pot plants which stood in a row on one side of the spacious reception area.

Anne, one of the receptionists, was speaking on the telephone and Gwenda at the other desk was busily slitting open envelopes with a formidable-looking paper knife. She looked up as the big door swung shut. 'Thank heaven you've arrived! Simon's like a bear with a sore head because you weren't here on the dot. I thought I'd open the mail to save time, and you'll find the messages on your pad.'

Jocelyn nodded her thanks as she walked towards the door leading into her own office, sparing a thought for the contrast between these luxurious premises and the offices Wadebridge's had occupied when they first opened for business. But there was no time now to admire her big desk, the expensive carpeting and other office furnishings, for the buzzer on the sophisticated intercom was making a noise like an angry wasp. Coming in with the morning's mail in her hand, Gwenda made an expressive grimace as she handed them over and Jocelyn gathered up the letters with her notebook and pencil before hurrying into Simon's inner sanctum.

'At last! I was beginning to think you'd decided to stay in bed this morning. Where have you been? Oh, never mind,' he went on before Jocelyn could explain. 'Now you are here at last, let's get on. Mother telephoned at an ungodly hour to tell me she and Candida were just taking off. Two cancellations came up at the last minute and they decided to take them. We'll have to get our skates on if we're to rearrange the reception committee, because it means they get in two hours earlier than planned.'

At once Jocelyn put everything out of her mind except the matter in hand. She would have first to let the national dailies know the change of plan, for the publicity of having persuaded a model as well known as Candida Melbourne to lead the forthcoming charity fashion show was too good to miss. It was also something of an honour that Wadebridge's had been asked to organize the occasion, which was to be held in a well known stately home. Royalty was to be present and several of the more famous designers were to show a wide range of day and evening clothes.

As she took down his instructions, Jocelyn could not help a twinge of admiration for Simon's seemingly inexhaustible energy. Moreover, he had the knack, she admitted grudgingly, of getting the best out of his employees. Not that anyone lasted long in this firm, she thought wryly, unless they pulled their weight, for Simon Wadebridge did not suffer fools gladly.

Getting up to return to her own office and make the first of a long list of telephone calls, she was brought to a halt when Simon suddenly said, 'You know, I rather like your hair short. Now why didn't Carl think of it before?' Then a frown appeared as his eyes slid over her. 'It's more than I can say for that outfit. Mother's losing her touch.'

'She chose the style, not the colour. They could only get my size in brown.'

'That explains it. Give the thing away. It might suit that girl you live with, but brown does absolutely nothing for you. Stick to your usual blues and greens – yes, and black. You look great in black.'

Jocelyn was too accustomed to Simon's blunt criticisms to let this one trouble her and she merely nodded before reaching out to open the door. But again Simon's voice made her stop as he called, 'Jocelyn!' There was a question as well as amusement in his tone as she turned with some surprise. 'Don't you ever feel like rebelling? Telling me to go to the devil?'

As she stood in startled silence Simon laughed outright. 'Never mind. Go and make those calls. If there isn't a barrage of cameras when Milady arrives she'll most likely turn round and go straight home.'

What a surprising man he was, Jocelyn thought as she

picked up her telephone. She began to alter the carefully planned preparations for Candida Melbourne's arrival which last night had seemed so successfully tied up and was just concluding a conversation with the manager of the hotel where their transatlantic guest was to stay when Simon came striding out of his office.

Impatiently he waited for her to finish speaking and as soon as she replaced her receiver to tick the list on the desk before her he asked abruptly, 'Was that the last?'

As Jocelyn nodded he added, 'Good – then I'd better get off myself. If there's a build-up of traffic between here and Heathrow it may take me some time to get to the airport and if I'm not there waiting when the plane touches down it might take some explaining.' He smiled suddenly, all his former brusqueness gone in a flash. 'Thanks, Jocelyn. You're a good child,' and slipping her list into his pocket, he was gone.

For several minutes Jocelyn sat motionless, her head resting on a cupped hand, staring at the closed door. She felt certain she would never understand Simon's abrupt changes in mood. He rarely praised or handed out thanks, and to follow it with a smile which turned up one corner of his shapely mouth was a bonus which seldom came her way. His behaviour was really so unusual that she felt vaguely uneasy. Impatience one moment and charm the next was not a combination to reassure a girl like herself.

At that moment Anne put her head round the door and broke into Jocelyn's contemplation as she asked, 'Feel like some coffee, Jo? I didn't dare interrupt until I knew Simon had gone. Gwenda and I had ours ages ago, but I've made fresh.'

Jocelyn smiled. 'I'd love a cup. Mrs. Wadebridge and Miss Melbourne are arriving earlier than we thought, hence all the panic, but now Simon's gone to meet them we can relax for the moment. I'll let you have some letters in about twenty minutes, meantime I'd like you to get on with the lists I left in your "in" basket last night. When they're ready, let me read them through.'

She was just putting down her empty cup when a slight man in his early thirties put in an appearance. 'I was looking for Simon. Not left already, has he?'

Jocelyn smiled as she nodded. She liked Walter Hook, the firm's accountant, for he was invariably pleasant and uncomplicated. He might appear nondescript with his mousy hair and pale blue eyes, but he was a financial wizard with a mind like an adding machine. Simon's maxim was 'if you can't do the job yourself, get someone who can', and since he paid high salaries to his senior employees he could afford someone like Walter.

Jocelyn often thought Simon only kept her on because she had been in the firm from the beginning. With only a small working capital Simon and his mother had been at first obliged to combine several jobs between them, and as well as secretary, Jocelyn herself had been receptionist, telephonist and often tea girl. But with Simon's drive and his mother's expertise in beauty culture all that had soon changed. The agency was well known now not only for being a good training school but also for spotting a potentially talented model before she had set foot on a catwalk.

Frequently these days the advertising agencies consulted Wadebridge's before their schemes were even on paper, and many established girls in the modelling field were only too happy to let Simon handle the business side of their careers. Jocelyn had to admit that Simon deserved most of the credit for the rapid success of the agency. When he pleased he could radiate a magic to which even the most temperamental girls succumbed.

Mrs. Wadebridge might expect the credit for having persuaded Candida Melbourne to appear at the charity function, but it was Jocelyn's secret opinion that Candida, who had met Simon briefly last year when he visited America, merely wanted a closer look at him. What better excuse than the charity show? Mrs. Wadebridge had phoned to say Candida had needed some persuasion, but it was possible that she was just playing hard to get. She was probably too clever a girl to show her hand this early in the game.

Jocelyn had seen too many beautiful girls nearly swoon with excitement when Simon turned on his not inconsiderable charm to be under any delusions. Some of the more sophisticated hid their enchantment better than others, but Jocelyn was too used to the signs to mistake them. Whether Simon himself felt anything like real warmth for any one of the ravishingly captivating girls who floated in and out of his life it was difficult to say. He was nearly thirty, apparently quite content with the single state, and still shared a home with his widowed mother, though they now occupied a comfortable flat within easy walking distance of the agency offices instead of the semi-detached which adjoined Jocelyn's family home.

But there was nothing captivating about the man standing patiently and quietly by her desk. Walter was nice, Jocelyn thought, and what a damning phrase that could be! She smiled up to find him watching her. 'He should have been here,' she explained, 'but we're in something of a state of chaos owing to Mrs. Wadebridge taking an early plane. Anything I can do, Walter?'

'Apart from having dinner with me, I should say not,' he smiled down. 'I suppose the answer's no as usual,' he said as he turned to the door. Jocelyn was glad she didn't in fact have to make the actual refusal as he went on, 'Tell Simon the auditors are coming next Tuesday, will you?' and the door closed silently behind him as Jocelyn made a note on her pad.

It was lunchtime before she recalled the letter which had arrived for her that morning. Reluctantly she opened her bag and took out the envelope. The contents confirmed her worst suspicions. Without preliminaries or proper explanations Alan asked for a loan, but it was the size of the amount he asked for which made Jocelyn push away her half-eaten meal, all appetite gone.

Where did he think she was to raise the five hundred pounds he urgently needed? And why, oh, why couldn't Alan keep out of trouble? she thought despairingly. She had always come to his rescue whenever possible because she put down most of his shortcomings to the fact that he had only been fourteen when their mother died.

Her replacement by a stepmother a year later hadn't helped. Janice, her older sister, had promptly married her childhood sweetheart and moved to Bristol, and Alan had never recovered from the traumatic experience of seeing a stranger in his beloved mother's place. Jocelyn had taken to Margaret, even sympathized with her difficulties in taking on a ready-made family of three, but she was the only one who had. On the point of leaving school however when her father remarried, she gladly accepted the chance to become independent when Mrs. Wadebridge offered her a job, despite the fact that this would bring her into close contact with Simon. As the big boy next door he had always given her a feeling of inadequacy.

Walter Hook was lounging in the one armchair her office boasted going through a set of figures when she returned from her lunch hour. He looked up and grinned as she walked in. 'The circus has started! Simon has been on to say the flowers for his mother and Miss Melbourne didn't arrive on time at the airport and that two of the photographers went to meet the wrong plane by mistake and will you ring and get them to go round to the hotel at five o'clock to get pictures for their morning editions. Oh, and contact Basil Beavis at *Ladies' Graces* and say Miss Melbourne will gladly give an interview, but can it wait for a couple of days? She's suffering from jet lag and not up to seeing anyone.'

Jocelyn laughed reluctantly, for Walter's face was wearing a decidedly sceptical expression. 'Not too tired to go with Simon to the ball tonight, though, I take it,' she replied, referring to the elaborate arrangements already made for Candida Melbourne to put in an appearance that evening at a ball in aid of the British Red Cross. It was taking place with what Simon himself had described as 'a heaven-sent convenience' just on the very day he wanted to show Candida off and would provide an additional and free announcement of her arrival in London.

Walter got to his feet. 'I know you refused dinner earlier, but wouldn't you like to come too and watch the fun?' he suggested half idly, half in earnest. 'I can easily get two more tickets.'

Jocelyn shook her head, for she had long ago decided Walter was too nice a person to string along. 'By the time I've done all the commissions from Simon plus what Gwenda and Anne have been saving up during my lunch break, I'll be lucky if I get away at seven o'clock, by which time I certainly won't feel like tripping the light fantastic, even to watch Candida taking the town by storm. Though it would have been nice to go and see her in action. Thank you for asking me,' Jocelyn added, and smiled to take the edge off her refusal as Walter without another word left her to get on with her work.

She watched the closed door for a moment or two, wishing she had felt able to accept his offer. Sighing, she picked up the telephone and two minutes later all recollection of Walter's invitation was erased from her mind as she concentrated on the afternoon's problems. But over supper that evening, the topic of the ball and Candida Melbourne came up again.

Jocelyn managed to get away earlier than anticipated and arrived home to find Janey dishing up an appetizing looking casserole. 'Good. I was hoping you'd be home in time to share this,' Janey said as Jocelyn threw her coat over a chair and came to help her friend carry in the hot dishes.

'Um, it smells good – what is in it?'

'Just about everything,' Janey answered, and laughed. 'Not knowing exactly what time that tyrant would let you off the hook, I popped all sorts of bits and pieces into the casserole. By the way, talking of Simon, take a look at that,' and she pushed over the evening paper.

Jocelyn found herself staring at a photograph of a triumphantly smiling girl holding Simon tightly by the arm. Mrs. Wadebridge had undoubtedly been standing beside them when the photograph was taken, but the paper had chosen to reproduce it as a cosy twosome. The letterpress beneath announced 'Famous Cover Girl Miss Candida Melbourne caught as she was met at Heathrow Airport by Mr. Simon Wadebridge. Miss Melbourne denied rumours of a romance and stated that they were just good friends.'

Free from the pressures at the agency offices, Jocelyn let out a delighted laugh. 'It's marvellous publicity, but how furious Simon will be when he sees it! Oh, he pretends it leaves him cold when reporters let their imaginations run riot, but underneath the apparent unconcern I know he detests speculation about his private life.'

'In my opinion it's his own fault if there are rumours,' Janey remarked dryly as she dished out generous portions of her stew. 'Heaven knows he asks for it.'

'By remaining single?' Jocelyn asked as she cut bread and handed a slice across the table to Janey. 'Surely it's his own affair if he wants to play the field. Though I must say,' she added thoughtfully, 'I never can understand the fascination he appears to exercise. Girls are continually throwing themselves at him, and to do Simon justice, usually without much encouragement.'

Janey paused with a forkful of food half-way to her mouth. 'Yet you're still immune. Does he never turn on the charm for you? I wonder why not?' Janey's observations were becoming embarrassing, so Jocelyn turned the conversation by drawing her friend's attention to another item of news in the paper. Not even to her long-time friend and confidante did she want to acknowledge that if Simon ever displayed a personal interest she would feel more uncomfortable than flattered. She had known him a long time, yet he still remained something of an enigma, and for some reason which she could not even explain to herself, she hoped Simon would continue to treat her simply as a useful piece of office furniture.

When Janey had gone on duty and the dishes were washed, Jocelyn took out Alan's letter and re-read the disturbing contents. Short of telling her father she could think of no way to raise the money Alan said he needed. But Jack Ashtead had left his only son in no doubt when he had run up debts his first year at college in Yorkshire that this was the only time he was going to come to his rescue. One person who might be willing to help, Jocelyn thought, was Simon's mother. Betty Wadebridge had been fond of their mother.

But on reaching the office next morning, Jocelyn discovered that any chance for a private conversation with Mrs. Wadebridge was out of the question. Simon buzzed before she had hung up her coat and Jocelyn found him looking through some documents which, judging from the frown on his face, did not make pleasing reading.

He glanced up as the door clicked to and motioned her to a chair. Superficially, Simon Wadebridge gave no indication of having a dynamic personality. It was only when he looked directly at you, Jocelyn thought, and it was possible to catch a glimpse of a shrewdly businesslike determination behind the grey eyes that one could begin to understand why he had so quickly made a name in a competitive and sometimes difficult field. Today he was dressed in a quiet grey suit with blue shirt and grey and black figured tie, and as he bent over his papers Jocelyn noticed how the dark brown hair curled over his ears and neck.

He wasn't strictly speaking a good-looking man, Jocelyn thought before she was jolted out of her silent contemplation of the brown-faced man on the other side of the desk by a sudden stream of instructions. Accustomed as she was to Simon's abrupt bursts of activity, her pencil automatically travelled smoothly across her notebook as he rapped out orders. Despite a busy day yesterday his face bore no sign of fatigue and he even threw her a brief smile as she got up, adding, 'By the way, Mother won't be in today. The trip's taken it out of her and I told her to stay in bed this morning. Perhaps you'll deal with anything that she usually sees to.'

Without waiting for a reply Simon nodded dismissal. Back in her own office, Jocelyn picked up the telephone, smoothing the skirt of the neat navy blue outfit she was wearing as she waited for her connection. Simon hadn't even noticed that she had complied with his order not to wear brown. Really, he deserved to be consigned to the devil, she thought, for he took her submission to his autocratic decrees far too much for granted.

She was gazing discontentedly at her reflection as she freshened her make-up prior to lunch when a draught made her look up. There were three doors in the room. One led into Simon's inner suite, one to the reception area and the third to a private corridor and exit only used by Simon and his mother. Jocelyn immediately recognized the girl who had used this private entrance and was now walking towards the inner office.

Moving quickly to intercept her, Jocelyn had time to admire the flawless complexion and shining chestnut hair as she said, 'I'm sorry, Miss Melbourne, but Mr. Wadebridge can't be disturbed.'

This was the first time she had seen Candida Melbourne in the flesh, and her breath caught in her throat at the sheer beauty of the girl in the mint green dress and matching wedge-heeled sandals who was eyeing her with obvious impatience. She flashed Jocelyn a brief smile,

17

patted her arm as if she were a rather obtuse child and drawled, 'Honey, that doesn't apply to me,' and brushing aside Jocelyn's detaining hand she opened the door to Simon's office, saying as she did so, 'Here I am, lover. I told you I'd be up by lunchtime. Now have you booked a table? I hear the Black Tulip's the place to go over here these days.'

Jocelyn forced an apologetic smile to her face as Simon got slowly to his feet and his eyes met hers over Candida's shoulder. There would be a reprimand, she felt sure, but with an 'All right, Jocelyn,' he dismissed her, and breathing a sigh of relief she escaped. It seemed odd, she thought, that he had not told her of Candida's probable arrival. Was it possible that he was as surprised as herself? It wasn't like, Simon, however to be caught out, and as she hurried off to lunch, Jocelyn wondered how he would cope with the situation. With excellent finesse and diplomacy, she felt certain.

Returning an hour later, she was not unduly surprised to hear the sound of occupancy in the inner office and putting her head round the door discovered Simon hard at work. An empty plate and glass on the desk revealed that he had had a working lunch and as he glanced up Jocelyn stammered an apology for disturbing him, adding, 'Sorry about the earlier interruption. Miss Melbourne didn't give me a chance to buzz you.'

Simon smiled, and expecting his normal impatient nod Jocelyn blinked. 'Think no more about it. I'm glad you're back; there are one or two things I want to tell you. Come in and shut the door.'

Jocelyn hovered as she replied, 'I'll just get my notebook,' and Simon immediately frowned irritably as he barked, 'You don't need a notebook. For goodness' sake do as you're told! Close the door and come and sit down. And stop looking as if I'm about to eat you. Sometimes I think if it weren't for Mother you'd hand me your notice.'

Jocelyn smiled as she slid into a chair, for Simon sounded almost resentful. 'She has been very good to me,' she volunteered shyly by way of excuse.

'Meaning I haven't?' he asked, and then as Jocelyn sat in tongue-tied silence waiting for his next broadside Simon suddenly swivelled the big armchair so that his back was turned as he stared through the window.

Sitting bolt upright in her chair, Jocelyn could not help wondering at this unusual behaviour. It was most un-characteristic of Simon to be hesitant. When he finally swung back to face her she felt she must be imagining the almost shy look in his eyes as he said abruptly, 'Mother's absence isn't only due to travel fatigue. She's given me quite a surprise, and a bit of a problem along with it. You remember her trip to visit Susan last year?' Jocelyn nodded, recalling how rejuvenated Betty Wadebridge had been on her return from visiting her married daugh-ter in Washington. 'Apparently Susan introduced her to a widowed colleague of my brother-in-law and while Mother was in New York this time, he flew up and asked her to marry him.'

'And has your mother accepted?' Jocelyn could not hide her delight at the unexpected news.

'All very well for you to look so starry-eyed,' Simon grumbled, though he too smiled as he went on, 'Now I've to decide what happens next, because apparently they want to get married soon. You've been doing Mother's jobs recently — apart from the make-up classes, of course. Think it will be too big a load to go on doing it indefinitely? Oh, I'll get a qualified beautician, of course, and another office girl, but could you manage the rest?'

Jocelyn was silent for half a minute, gazing out of the window behind Simon in her turn as she thought the matter out. Coming to a sudden decision, she turned to find him watching her intently. His grey eyes, so similar in colour to her own, held an anxious expression, and that look gave her confidence. Jocelyn smiled, unaware of the pleasing picture she presented to the man behind the big leather-topped desk.

'I think I could cope. Anne and Gwenda are very good. They can do the more routine things standing on their heads.'

'That's settled, then. Promote Gwenda to your office and get another girl for reception. I leave it to you.'

Jocelyn knew she must have imagined his sigh of relief, for as she started to rise Simon said peremptorily, 'Don't go. I've another request to make and I may as well get it over now as later. When Mother leaves, will you take her place in my home as well as here? Come and live with me at the flat?'

As a look of total disbelief spread across Jocelyn's face he added with a crooked smile, 'As my wife, of course.'

Jocelyn felt a wave of pure anger surge through her and pushing back the chair she forgot for a second her usual fear of Simon's reactions. 'If that was a joke, it was in very bad taste!'

Simon got to his feet and walking round the desk possessed himself of Jocelyn's hand, holding it between his own warm palms. 'I don't make jokes with people I respect, Jocelyn. I mean it. I'd consider myself very honoured if you could bring yourself to accept,' and he kissed the hand he was holding before releasing it.

Jocelyn glanced from Simon's intent face to her own hand as if she had never seen either before, and passing a tongue over her dry lips she struggled to reply. 'You must be out of your mind! If you're not joking then you must be doing this for a bet.' She almost ran in her haste to leave, ignoring Simon's 'Wait, please,' and scuttled to the doubtful sanctuary of the staff room.

Jocelyn spent ten minutes feverishly attending to her appearance in an effort to master the butterflies in her tummy which Simon's extraordinary proposal had produced. No, she told herself, as she applied more lipstick with trembling fingers, marriage with Simon was quite unthinkable. She had to acknowledge that he had placed her in something of a dilemma, however. If she refused, would she still have a job, or did that also hinge on her answer?

When she finally crept out reluctantly from her hiding place Gwenda greeted her with the news that Simon had left and would not be back for the rest of the afternoon, and Jocelyn, glad of the respite, applied herself to her duties. At least she didn't have to face a rejected suitor, if one could call Simon that, until tomorrow morning. Meantime she determined to go and visit her father, for Alan's pressing need for money had still to be solved.

When she walked round to the back door of her old home later that evening, Jocelyn could see her stepmother busy in the kitchen. Margaret Ashtead turned and smiled a welcome when she saw the visitor and Jocelyn went across to kiss her cheek.

'I hope you can stay for supper,' Margaret said as she went on with the cooking. 'Janice and the children are here. Mark's mother had a stroke last night and they drove up from Bristol first thing this morning. Mark and his father are still at the hospital, but Jan's come home to put the little ones to bed.'

As she finished speaking the kitchen door opened and Jocelyn's older sister entered, her tired face lighting up as she saw the figure at the kitchen table. 'I was going to phone you when the children were asleep,' she said after they had embraced. 'There hasn't been a minute all day. Mrs. Bury isn't expected to last the night, so I stayed at the hospital as long as I could.'

While voicing her condolences, Jocelyn was wondering whether in the circumstances she would get a chance of five minutes alone with her father. During supper, however, it was brought home to her that there was little to be gained in trying to get help for Alan here. A chance inquiry from Janice as to whether anyone had heard recently from him brought a bitter retort from Jack

Ashtead that since every communication from his son contained a demand for money he was thankful not to have had a letter. 'Since he took up with that Christopher Tenby he's worse, and I'm throwing no more good money away. All I hope is he hasn't been borrowing elsewhere.'

'Not much chance of touching Mark and me,' Janice laughed. 'After we've paid the mortgage and running expenses we're lucky if we get one evening out a month for some entertainment. Alan knows he'd be unlucky coming to us for a loan.'

Jocelyn kept quiet, dreading every moment that her silence would give her away, and on the train going back to her flat she could think of nothing else except how she was to answer her brother's letter. But a couple of seconds after putting her key into the lock it was plain that Alan hadn't waited for a reply. She found Janey feeding him and his college friend Christopher Tenby with coffee and sandwiches, and a few moments' conversation revealed that they had brought sleeping bags and intended staying the night.

As they were clearing away Jocelyn managed a whispered apology to Janey. 'I'd no idea Alan intended coming tonight, otherwise I'd never have gone over to see Dad and Margaret,' but Janey Rushwick had known Alan for too long to be surprised by his unexpected appearance. 'Not to worry. They didn't walk in until nearly ten o'clock. I only hope he hasn't come for more of your savings. You're a fool to keep lending every time he asks. Time he learned to live on his grant.'

Jocelyn wondered what Janey would say if she knew Alan's demands on this particular occasion. She had only started cleaning off her make-up when, after a light tap, Alan slid quietly into her room and threw himself on to the bed. Jocelyn waited, watching his reflection curiously in the mirror as she wiped her face and neck with a handful of tissues.

There was a half wary, half crafty expression on her brother's face, Jocelyn noted sadly, and she wondered why he had turned out such a weakling, easily led astray by people like Christopher Tenby. Jocelyn had taken an instinctive dislike to her brother's latest crony, heightened by his smarmy manner and the way he watched Janey when he thought no one was looking.

She was brought out of these unwelcome thoughts by Alan asking, 'You got my letter, I suppose?'

Jocelyn swivelled round on the stool to face him. 'How can you need so much, Alan? What's it for? You must know I can't raise that amount.'

Alan looked anywhere but at her face, a sulky expression marring his features as his eyes slid round the room avoiding his sister's honest eyes. 'It's a long story, Jo. Got into debt playing poker, if you must know. Got to pay them soon.'

'Who's they, and have you been in trouble gambling before?'

Alan's eyes were now half shut as he leaned back full length on Jocelyn's bed. 'Crowd at college,' he replied, ignoring the second question. 'Couple of fellows run a poker game once a week. Strictly against the rules, of course. Probably get expelled if they were caught.'

'Then this isn't the first time you've played?' Jocelyn asked.

'No, and don't look so righteous, for goodness' sake. You're as bad as Dad,' Alan burst out as he looked across and caught the expression on his sister's face.

'So Dad bailed you out last time. That's why he said tonight that you'd had your last penny out of him, I suppose.'

Alan sat bolt upright at her words. 'You never told him about the five hundred?'

Jocelyn picked up her hairbrush. 'Of course not.' She began to brush her hair vigorously. 'I can't possibly raise all that, so I went down to see if he'd help. Janice is at home, so I never had the chance of a word alone with him. Mark's mother is ill, the whole family are up staying with Dad and Margaret. During supper it popped out that you'd already borrowed from them and Dad said he hoped Jan and I wouldn't lend you money.'

'What am I going to do?' Alan pleaded. 'Chris says I must find the money somehow.'

'If he knows so much about this gang he's probably one of them,' Jocelyn said tartly, and Alan jumped to his feet.

'That's right, blame Chris! You never liked him.'

'No, because I think he's a bad influence. Tell me, how did you hear of this poker club? I'd bet my last penny Christopher Tenby introduced you to it.'

The answer was on Alan's face, and Jocelyn sighed. 'Let me sleep on it,' she said wearily, for already a desperate remedy to get Alan out of his latest predicament had occurred to her. All she had to decide was whether she had the courage to go through with it.

After lying awake for what seemed like hours, practising how she might broach the subject, Jocelyn was still undecided on how she was going to put her plan into action. It would not be easy to tell any man, but especially Simon, that in exchange for your hand if not your heart you wanted cash on the nail even before the wedding ring was safely in place. It was therefore in something of a quandary that Jocelyn arrived next morning at the agency.

Mrs. Wadebridge had already arrived, and in the excitement of greeting her and congratulating her on her forthcoming marriage, Jocelyn almost forgot her own dilemma and yesterday's alarms and excursions. The morning proceeded in its usual pattern until just before one o'clock Candida Melbourne swept in, much as she had done the day before, to throw open the door leading into Simon's office without so much as a 'by your leave'.

Five minutes later Jocelyn received the special signal

from Simon's intercom. and three minutes later Mrs. Wadebridge entered with a male companion and went into the inner office.

Alone again, Jocelyn grinned. Operation 'Save my skin' was once more about to be put into operation, and she felt a faint pang of pity for the beautiful Candida. It was a plan Simon and Mrs. Wadebridge had long ago perfected to relieve him of unwelcome visitors and for success relied on sheer simplicity. Mrs. Wadebridge would simply arrive accompanied by the best-looking male model currently working at the agency. Soon even the most persistent hanger-on would find herself swept off to partake of a lavish lunch before realization could dawn that she had been the victim of a well laid plan.

It had never failed before, and today was no exception. It could not have been more than ten minutes later before a companionable threesome left Simon's office, and he even came to open the door to reception, saying as Candida passed, 'Sorry about this, but I'll see you this evening.'

It was unlike Simon to risk upsetting such a valuable if temporary acquisition as Candida, and Jocelyn felt frankly puzzled by his behaviour, but the answer was simple. Going in in answer to his buzz, Jocelyn discovered him standing in the doorway of the cloakroom leading out of his office preparing to leave for lunch. 'Get your bag. I'm taking you for a ploughman's lunch at the pub. I hadn't time to go chasing you yesterday, but we've something to get settled,' he said without preamble. So that was it, Jocelyn thought as she went to tidy herself. Business before pleasure. Single-minded Simon wanted things cut and dried. How typical too that it had simply not occurred to him that she might already have made alternative arrangements for her lunch hour. If it had, presumably he expected her to jettison them for his benefit at a moment's notice.

Jocelyn bit her resentment back. For Alan's sake at

least she must hide all signs of offence. Hadn't her own mother always told her one could get more by using honey than vinegar? Jocelyn hid her vexation behind a bright smile as Simon ushered her out of the building to stroll to the old pub tucked up a side alley five minutes' walk away.

They discussed the forthcoming show until sandwiches, bread, cheese and drinks had been set on their small table in a quiet corner of the bar. As he dealt hungrily with a chunk of crisply baked bread and a hunk of Cheshire cheese, Simon said softly, 'Thought any more about marrying me?'

Jocelyn shot him a scared glance, a ham sandwich halfway to her mouth, and swallowed. Here came the crunch. She blurted out her answer baldly, all the flowery sentences she had rehearsed last night eluding her as she faced this sharp-eyed man. 'Yes, and I'll do it if you'll let me have five hundred pounds right away.'

There was a moment's stunned silence before Simon began to laugh. His reaction startled Jocelyn so much she let the sandwich drop from her trembling fingers as she whispered, 'Don't make fun, Simon. It's not fair. Didn't you mean it after all?'

Simon controlled his laughter with an obvious effort and replied quickly, his grey eyes still crinkled with amusement.

'You must know me well enough by now, otherwise I'd not have dragged you out to lunch. Of course I meant it. But it's not every day one's future bride asks for a loan before the happy man has had time to even congratulate himself on his good fortune. Alan again, I suppose. Or is Janice in the red this time?'

Trust Simon to guess the truth right away! She could not meet the sardonic mischief in the eyes watching her as she answered, 'Of course it's not Janice. You know what a careful person Mark is. He'd no more dream of getting into debt than the man in the moon.'

'So it is Alan?' This time there was no laughter but a grim note in Simon's deep voice. 'Pity your father didn't belt him more when he had the chance. Oh yes, I know all about the psychological effect of your mother's death,' he went on as he saw Jocelyn open her lips to interrupt. 'Just the same, I think your brother would have responded better to a spanking now and then instead of all that psychiatric nonsense. Why didn't he go to your father to get him out of his difficulties, by the way?'

Jocelyn looked up at this, unconscious pleading in the depths of the big grey eyes. 'Dad says he's not going to help Alan any more, but I can't turn my back, Simon. Really I can't. If you won't give me the money I don't know what I'll do.'

'You might take back your promise to marry me, and I can't have that. Leave Alan to me – I'll handle him. Where is he? At college or drifting about London until he can lay his hands on the money one way or another?'

'He's at the flat,' Jocelyn mumbled, then added, 'You won't . . .' she hesitated.

'No, I won't flatten him, much as he deserves it. Just see he learns a few home truths. I've noticed your obvious unhappiness whenever he was up in London. Trouble is, your mother spoiled him rotten. Come on, drink up. While you go back to the office I'll sort out your young brother. The sooner he's out of your hair the better.'

Simon left Jocelyn outside the agency, having first obtained her flat key. He returned it to her an hour later, dropping it casually on to her desk as he walked past to go into his own office and silencing Jocelyn's questions by bidding her tell Walter Hook to come and see him. Simon's face bore its usual calm, unapproachable expression and she was forced to thrust down all the questions bubbling inside.

The rest of the afternoon flew by with scarcely a breather for anyone on Simon's immediate staff. Walter was closeted with him for well over an hour and afterwards a succession of visitors and telephone calls prevented Jocelyn from getting even a moment's privacy with her unpredictable employer. She was locking her desk and preparing to leave when he came out into her office and said briefly, 'Ring and tell your family the news. I'll break the glad tidings to Mother when I've dropped Candida off. By the way, I shall want you to take her over to Pendleton tomorrow morning for some photographs. Apparently she wouldn't permit the photographer from *Ladies' Graces* to snap her this afternoon when she was interviewed, so warn one of the girls to stand in for you tomorrow morning.' He stood looking down into her questioning eyes. 'Yes, I gave him the money, so relax,' and he strode out.

So much for romance, Jocelyn thought as she wrote a note to leave on Gwenda's desk. Your fiancé taking out another girl before you've even time to announce one's engagement!

Silence greeted her as she pushed open the front door. Janey was not due back, but she had half expected Alan and Christopher to still be around. They had apparently departed bag and baggage. No odd sock under a chair, forgotten toothbrush or even a note of thanks. As Jocelyn went to look over the contents of the fridge she thought Alan might at least have left her a message, but once she had arranged his financial problem he probably forgot her very existence. In his own way he was as single-minded as Simon. This was Janey's last night off duty and Jocelyn was surprised when the front door banged and her friend came into the kitchen. 'Got enough for two?' she asked. 'George has had to go on duty as they're short-staffed in Casualty.' George Yate, a young doctor, had been Janey's steady boy-friend for some months.

'I wondered why you'd come home so early,' Jocelyn replied as she put another lamb chop under the griller and rapidly calculated that the vegetables she had prepared would stretch to two portions.

'We'd arranged to go to that new film at the Odeon too,' Janey said gloomily as she laid the table. 'Alan gone back to college? They were still sleeping when I went out.'

'Apparently,' Jocelyn answered shortly as the two girls sat down to eat their evening meal, but her mind was not on her brother's possible whereabouts. It had suddenly occurred to her that not only would her family be surprised at her forthcoming marriage but that explaining it to Janey was not going to be easy. As she reached for the mint sauce she said, 'I've something to tell you. Simon Wadebridge asked me to marry him yesterday.'

Janey's reaction was unexpected, for she put down her knife and fork and looking across the table burst out laughing. 'So you may be immune to him, but apparently he isn't immune to you! How incredible,' she went on. 'All the time you've been trembling at the knees scared to death of him he's been nurturing a secret passion.'

'It's not like that at all,' Jocelyn, honest to the bone, couldn't let her oldest friend be taken in. 'His mother's getting married again, to an American. Simon merely wants a replacement.'

'You refused, of course.' Janey, her eyes twinkling, went on with supper, but her head jerked up as Jocelyn answered dolefully, 'No, I said I would.'

'Jo, honestly – you must be out of your tiny mind! Why, only the other day you swore you weren't in the least interested in Simon. Oh, I know he can offer you lots in material ways, but a spot of the fluttery heart feeling comes in useful in marriage, so I'm told. It would never work if you're dead scared of the guy. When George kisses me I hear bells ringing. What do you feel when Simon kisses you?'

'I don't know. He's never kissed me,' Jocelyn said, and then as Janey opened her mouth she added, 'It's no good, I've got to do it, Janey. You were right about Alan needing money. He wanted rather a lot – more than Dad

29

could have afforded even if he'd been willing to help. Simon's fixed it up.'

'You're taking the sisterly martyr act rather far, aren't you?' Janey asked, then as Jocelyn pushed her meal away only half eaten added quickly, 'Don't do it, Jo! Surely Simon would just lend you the money if you asked him. You could repay it a bit at a time.'

'Do you think he would?' Jocelyn asked hopefully.

'No harm in asking,' Janey replied as she put out cheese and biscuits, set coffee on the table. 'Where is Sir Galahad, by the way?'

'Taking Candida Melbourne to a cocktail party.' Jocelyn's tones were so gloomy that at Janey's burst of laughter she smiled ruefully. 'It was arranged some days ago.'

Janey stirred sugar into her coffee and between chuckles said, 'Honestly, you're too good to be true. I don't know of another girl who'd let herself be trampled on by the men in her life like you do. You should have insisted on Simon taking you for a celebration drink at the very least, even though the engagement is all on Alan's account. What do the family think about it?'

'I haven't told them yet.'

'Still time to get out of it, then,' announced practical Janey. 'First thing tomorrow tell Simon you've changed your mind. If he's already handed over the money he can hardly refuse to make it a loan.'

To prevent more discussion about her engagement, Jocelyn turned Janey's thoughts to other matters. Over the washing-up she said, 'You know I've got to help out at the show tomorrow night? Trouble is I don't know what to wear. I expect Mrs. Wadebridge will want me on hand backstage for emergencies that might crop up, but there's a buffet supper and dancing afterwards, so it will have to be something formal. I don't want to let the side down.'

'Wear your halter-neck chiffon, then, with the matching jacket. It's just the job. You'll look lovely – formal but not overdressed. When the dancing starts you can discard your jacket and then that neckline and low back will really come into its own. You've lovely shoulders. Pity you don't get more chances to show them off.'

'Thanks, you do marvels for a girl's ego,' Jocelyn laughed. 'I'll have to change at the office, though. Tomorrow will be so busy, I just know, and there'll be no time to come back here.'

Jocelyn dressed with care next morning, choosing from her wardrobe a honey-coloured suit in a synthetic linen material which she teamed with a black blouse and accessories. If she were to take Candida to a photographic studio she might as well look her best, and there was also her forthcoming confrontation with Simon. It was all very well for Janey to say he could not refuse her request. Janey simply didn't know how his icy snubs could hurt. He was too used to people jumping promptly to do his bidding to take kindly to argument.

She arrived at the agency early and had all the outstanding routine jobs out of the way before Simon opened his door. He seemed surprised to see her and glanced at his watch. 'Not forgotten you're picking Candida up, I trust?' he asked urbanely, then as Jocelyn shook her head he went on, 'Good, then as you're still here will you get me Peter Dewsbury on the line?'

As he turned to go he asked, 'Were your folks surprised at our news?'

'I haven't told them. Simon . . .' Jocelyn's voice halted as she caught the look in his eyes. They wore what she privately called his 'cat and mouse' expression.

'Yes, and why not, may I inquire?' His tones were silky and inwardly Jocelyn shivered.

It was too late now to turn back. For good or ill she would have to go on, so quickly she blurted out, 'I was thinking last night – couldn't the money you've given Alan be just a loan? I'd pay you back as quickly as I could,' she added as something flickered at the back of

Simon's eyes.

'I'd never have guessed you'd default on an agreement,' he replied at last, then he flicked Jocelyn on the raw. 'You're more like Alan than I would have guessed.'

'That's not fair!' Jocelyn flared, and had no notion of how the rosy glow in her cheeks enhanced the elfin charm of her big grey eyes and new flyaway hairdo. 'You don't really want to be handicapped with a wife when you have a perfectly good housekeeper in Mrs. Telford to see to your every need,' she added, referring to the Wadebridges' daily help.

'I think I'm the best judge of that,' Simon replied softly, 'and since I've already told Mother we're getting married and have carried out my side of our bargain there's no more to be said. After all,' he remarked as a parting shot, 'if my memory serves me the bargain was your idea in the first place. Now may I suggest you ask Gwenda to make that call and get off to collect Candida?'

So much for Janey's brainwave Jocelyn thought wearily as she gathered up her handbag and set out for Candida Melbourne's hotel. She was surprised that Candida was not only up but ready and waiting, a vision of loveliness in a candy pink trouser suit, every inch of her a top flight model. Heads turned as the two girls went through the foyer to wait for a taxi – though not, Jocelyn thought dismally, because of me. She was well aware that her exchange with Simon had banished the last vestiges of her self-confidence. As she gave the address and followed Candida's graceful figure into the taxi she felt her spirits had reached rock bottom. It seemed she was irretrievably committed to marrying a man who would not hesitate to make her submit to his dictates.

CHAPTER TWO

On the way to Pablo Pendleton's studio Candida talked artlessly and amiably about her impact on London, and Jocelyn decided she was basically a nice girl, but like many models obsessed with her own appearance and career. As the taxi hurried them through the mid-morning traffic Jocelyn wondered what it felt like to be an accredited beauty, sought after and spoiled by constant adulation.

Was Simon blind to Candida's beauty? Surely not, otherwise he would not have gone to so much trouble to acquire her services as star of the show this evening. Maybe his secret was never to allow his heart to rule his head. That seemed a likely solution, for though he had to Jocelyn's certain knowledge enjoyed brief love affairs with one or another of the girls he met during the course of his business, yet it was herself, more useful than ornamental, to whom he had proposed marriage.

By the time they reached the mews where Pablo had his studio Jocelyn was indulging in an orgy of self-pity. She was roused from her thoughts by the sudden braking of the cab and Candida's bright, 'This must be it. Yes, I recognize the place from my visit last year. Pay the man, darling, while I go and announce myself.'

By the time the taxi driver had given Jocelyn her change she discovered Candida affectionately embracing a slight, dark-haired man clad in casual slacks and pullover. In the hubbub Jocelyn could not hear what he was saying, but she saw him tactfully disengage himself from Candida's arms, call over one of his assistants and then turn to make his way across the many cables and lighting equipment with which the room was littered to reach Jocelyn's side.

'Go on up. Angie's expecting you,' and he grinned and indicated the narrow staircase on the opposite side of the room which lead to the upper floor. 'You can safely leave Miss America in my capable hands.'

Jocelyn smiled as she took Pablo's advice. He was an unobtrusive man, quite the opposite of most people's idea of a famous photographer, and as well as being unsensational in appearance he had the reputation of being unfashionably faithful to his wife. Angie Pendleton was one of Jocelyn's close friends, the girls having met some years previously when Angie was a journalist. For the time being she had given up even freelance work to prepare for the imminent arrival of her first baby.

When Jocelyn reached the top of the stairs Angie called, 'If that's you, Jo, come into the kitchen. I'm making coffee.'

As soon as Jocelyn appeared in the doorway Angie said, 'Um, how slim you are! I must say I'm looking forward to getting my figure back. *And* see my feet for the first time for months.'

Jocelyn laughed. 'You're a fraud. You won't admit it but you're having the time of your life, and you and Pablo can't wait to be proud parents.'

'Agreed. Just the same, it will be nice to be eight stone again instead of nearly eleven, and you've no idea what those gorgeous creatures downstairs do to my self-esteem! Sometimes I wish Pablo were in any other business than this. The comparison when he comes upstairs and looks at a shapeless wife would turn lesser men green.'

As Jocelyn laughed at Angie's droll expression, her friend started to pour coffee into two mugs, saying as she did so, 'I had Simon on the telephone earlier. He tells me you two are going to be married. I'm so glad.'

'Thanks.' At a loss for words, Jocelyn flushed as she stirred cream into her coffee. 'Did he ... is he ...' She stopped and seeing Angie's surprised glance added, 'The fact is we only settled things yesterday and I haven't had

34

time to exchange more than half a dozen words with him this morning.' And what words, she thought as she went on. 'We have this show tonight. But of course you know – Pablo's doing the photographs. Are you coming?'

'Like this?' Angie gestured towards her ample figure. 'You must be kidding! However, I've invited Simon to come over for lunch. Pablo won't have finished the stuff for *Ladies' Graces* before then, so you may as well stay on.'

'I ought to get back. We've mountains of work,' Jocelyn protested halfheartedly.

'Nonsense, knowing Simon I'm sure everything is in apple-pie order, so stop fussing and help me get the meal ready. I've a veal casserole in the oven and the makings of a green salad in the fridge. What do you think the fair Candida would fancy for a sweet?'

'Nothing, if her figure is anything to go by,' Jocelyn smiled as she took off her jacket, but Angie wasn't so certain.

'These sylph-like creatures often eat like horses,' she commented, 'so don't bank on her being the black coffee and crispbread type. How do raspberry creams grab you?'

The two girls finished their coffee, then while Jocelyn laid the table Angie Pendleton put a concoction of thick cream, Kirsch, frozen raspberries and sugar into a blender before spooning the mixture into individual glasses and leaving them to chill.

Jocelyn and Angie were drinking aperitifs in the sitting-room when Simon Wadebridge put in an appearance. He carried two wrapped bottles as he advanced to kiss Angie's cheek and compliment her on her healthy appearance, then putting the bottles aside he sat down on the arm of Jocelyn's chair and took her hand. He was wearing what Jocelyn called his 'persuasive' smile as he asked, 'You didn't mind my telling Angie and Pablo our news, did you?' His eyes mocked as turning to Angie he said, 'I've brought some champagne. Mind if I put it in your fridge for half an hour?'

Releasing Jocelyn, he rose and went to cool the wine as Angie raised expressive brows. 'Doing you proud,' she hissed. 'What did the fair Candida say when she heard the news?'

Jocelyn was saved from answering by Simon's return. 'Pablo and Candida will be up in a minute or two. They were just on the last lap when I arrived, if you'll forgive the mixed metaphor.'

He had hardly finished speaking when Pablo pushed the door wide, ushering Candida in front of him.

'What's this about laps?' he asked as he caught the last part of Simon's conversation.

'Not mine anyway,' Angie answered him, her eyes on Candida, who had gone to lean possessively on Simon's shoulder. 'It's non-existent at the moment. Give Candida a drink, Pablo, and don't take too long. The meal's nearly ready and the champagne is on ice.'

They exchanged glances before Pablo walked across to the drinks trolley, a smile playing about his mouth. In that one brief look a message had obviously passed from wife to husband, for as he handed drinks to Candida and Simon he said, 'Congratulations are in order, I hear. Sorry I didn't wish you luck downstairs when you arrived, Jo,' and in the most natural way in the world, Pablo leaned forward to place a congratulatory kiss on Jocelyn's cheek.

Candida looked from one to the other. 'What's going on? You're very mysterious.' There was bewilderment in the wide eyes.

Simon disengaged himself to walk over and take Jocelyn's hand in a warm clasp. 'No mystery, sweet. Jocelyn and I have just decided to make it official, that's all. We're going to be married in three weeks' time.'

'Married?' the usually soft accents held an almost strident note. 'You never told me you were engaged, lover.'

Simon smiled at Candida, a smile Jocelyn watched with curiosity, for beneath its charm she sensed guardedness. Then he turned to glance at his hosts, saying as he did so, 'This demure young lady stole my heart in her cradle. I've just been waiting for her to grow up.'

Candida pouted and turned her back pointedly to speak to Pablo, who had put a glass into her hand. Behind Candida's back, Angie grinned a friendly message of sympathy before getting to her feet to ask Pablo, 'Coming to help me dish up the meal, darling?'

He turned at once to follow his wife, leaving behind an uncomfortable silence which Simon made no attempt to break. Candida glanced once at the pair in the armchair, Jocelyn's fingers still hidden in Simon's larger hand, then picking up her bag she slung it over one shoulder and murmuring something about 'freshening up' she too closed the door behind her, leaving Simon and Jocelyn alone.

Immediately Simon released her and stood up. 'Feel like another drink?' he asked, while Jocelyn watched him warily. 'By the way, Mother was sorry to miss you this morning. She asked me to give you her love and says she'll wish us luck in person tonight. Your father seems pleased. I rang him at his office after you'd gone.'

A retort was wrung out of Jocelyn at this high-handedness. 'You might have let me break the news!'

'What, and risk you trying to chicken out again? No chance. Besides, it is usual to inform a father that you want to carry off his daughter.' Simon's smile was openly mocking. 'In any case, I wanted to make sure you didn't disregard my wishes a second time.'

'Don't I always do as you tell me sooner or later?' An unconsciously bitter note sounded in Jocelyn's usually soft voice. 'And I wasn't aware there were any definite plans for our wedding as yet. You said "in three weeks" just now.'

'You well know my methods. I like everything cut and

dried well in advance,' Simon repeated mockingly as she eyed him guardedly. 'We're going to be married quietly on the nineteenth of next month, which will give us time to have a few days to ourselves before Mother leaves for the States.'

Jocelyn gasped, for even experience of Simon's energy and drive had not prepared her for being swept into marriage quite so quickly. As if he could read her very thoughts Simon said softly, 'You know me – I never do something for nothing. I carried out my side of the bargain yesterday and see no reason why I should give you time to run out on me.'

'Do you think I would?' Jocelyn asked daringly, but she was so angry at Simon's insinuation that she forgot her usual self-consciousness when under his sharp eye. 'If you do I can't think why you want to marry me.'

Simon laughed as he walked over to pull her to her feet. 'Get off your high horse and come and eat. Angie will be beginning to imagine the worst.' But if Angie Pendleton had wondered why Jocelyn and Simon delayed before joining the others she gave no sign. She was sitting at the dining-table placidly ladling out enormous portions from a bubbling casserole while Pablo, who had opened the wine, was filling Candida's glass with the sparkling pink champagne.

The lunch went off smoothly, helped along by Simon and Pablo's effortless handling of the conversation, and by the time the meal ended Jocelyn had lost her shyness and even Candida seemed to have forgotten her earlier petulance. They were lingering over coffee when Simon looked at his watch. 'Better get going if we're to reach Petswood Castle by tea-time. I promised Mother we wouldn't be late. Are you coming in my car, Pablo, or taking your own?'

'I'll drive down in my own,' Pablo replied. 'Steve will have already loaded up. Like to come with us?' he asked, turning to Candida, but after a swift glance across the room at Simon she replied smoothly, 'Thanks, but I have to be there before you do. Why not give Jocelyn another cup of coffee, then you can give her a lift.'

'Sorry, no go,' Simon interrupted before Pablo could reply. 'We need Jocelyn as much as you, Candida my love. And don't worry about your evening things,' he added, anticipating Jocelyn's anxiety. 'I've put your bag in the boot with my own.'

Jocelyn, turning away, found Angie listening to the interchange with a look of amusement deep in her laughing eyes. 'My gosh, I wish I were able to come with you,' she remarked. 'Tonight could be interesting.' Jocelyn had no trouble in catching her friend's meaning, for Angie's sister had been a top model, just as beautiful but a good deal more temperamental than Candida Melbourne. Outside, seeing them off, she could not resist winking surreptitiously at Jocelyn when Candida got into the front passenger seat as a matter of course.

As Jocelyn turned to kiss her goodbye Angie whispered naughtily, 'May the best girl win!' which made Jocelyn get into the back of Simon's car with a smile touching her own lips at the sheer absurdity of the situation. As he adjusted the driving mirror, she suddenly discovered her eyes looking straight into Simon's. His reassuring glance before he switched on the engine did much to compensate her for the fact that during the journey Candida made no effort to include her in a low-toned conversation monopolising Simon's attention.

Jocelyn, watching first the London suburbs, then gradually the countryside flash by her window, shut her ears to the murmur of voices in front, for it gave her time to try and sort out her confused feelings. Even Simon's surprising disclosure of their engagement to the Pendletons didn't make it seem more real. Jocelyn wished she had nerve enough to stand up to Simon, ask him the true reasons behind his proposal of marriage. Perhaps his mother's second plunge into the matrimonial stakes had made him decide it was time he too took this important step. But he was scarcely in his dotage and this conclusion did not answer the all-important question of why he had chosen herself. He could and frequently did have his pick from a wide circle of fascinating women, though not one lasted for more than a few weeks. At the first sign of possessiveness, Simon's interest cooled overnight.

Was this perhaps the answer? Maybe he imagined the hard-working, self-effacing Jocelyn whom he had known since childhood would do very well as an easily manageable wife, one moreover who could combine the roles of secretary, hostess and agency manageress with that of being Mrs. Simon Wadebridge. She was still musing on Simon's possible motives when he turned the car into the imposing gateway of the stately home lent for the occasion.

From then on Jocelyn had little time for introspection, for inside the beautiful and historic house all seemed confusion. People were scurrying about without, it appeared, much proper teamwork, and soon Jocelyn found herself caught up in the general turmoil as people clashed either with each other or the resident staff.

The different ranges of garments, beachwear, lingerie, day and evening clothes were from a number of different designers and Mrs. Wadebridge lost no time in enlisting Jocelyn's help in running to ground the boxes containing the models from Jupiter Jove, a new name on the fashion scene, which had been delivered but so far had not reached the changing-rooms on the first floor. Jocelyn might often feel tongue-tied with Simon. Away from his unnerving presence, however, she was a different person and soon found her way to where a harassed housekeeper was trying to prevent one of the florist's assistants from placing a heavy stone urn on a priceless antique table.

Immediately the matter had been sorted out, Jocelyn claimed the housekeeper's help in locating the missing dress boxes, and these were eventually discovered in a study leading out of the entrance hall. There was no one to act as porter, so picking up the largest box, Jocelyn staggered in the direction of the dressing-rooms.

Upstairs a bevy of assistants were assembling the various garments and accessories, ironing those crushed in transit and generally making sure that everything was in pristine condition for the show later that evening. Models, some wearing light dressing-gowns, others scantily clad only in bra and panties, seemed everywhere, getting under people's feet as they assembled their make-up or clamoured for the attention of Carl and his assistant hairdressers who had driven down earlier with Mrs. Wadebridge. Downstairs, an orchestra was rehearsing, and the cacophony of sound, as the music added to the poise of caterers preparing the buffet plus shouting as people tried to make themselves heard above the general clamour, made Jocelyn wonder whether everything would be ready by the time the first guests put in an appearance.

Gradually, however, order grew out of the chaos. The florists finished transforming the lower floor and staircase into a bower of flowers, members of the orchestra departed for refreshment, the clatter of glasses, plates and cutlery ceased as the long tables stood ready to serve the expected crowd. Even on the upper floor it was comparatively quiet as everyone took a breather while they had the opportunity.

Candida Melbourne was amongst those who seemed only too happy to find time to take a rest, for she sat lacquering her nails, looking as cool as the proverbial cucumber. Some of the girls, however, showed signs of nerves and Jocelyn stayed to dispense tea or coffee and calm the first sign of stage fright while Simon and Mrs. Wadebridge changed into their evening attire.

Betty Wadebridge returned some thirty minutes later looking almost as glamorous as her charges in a simple gown of a diaphanous blue-grey material covered by a floor-length matching coat. Her eyes lit with pleasure as

Jocelyn said admiringly, 'You look lovely. Is it new?'

Mrs. Wadebridge's eyes twinkled. 'Part of my trousseau, actually, but I couldn't resist wearing it tonight. Pray that no one drops anything on it. Off you go. I've given Simon the lists, but he wants you downstairs as soon as possible so he can use you as messenger should he have to change the order.'

Jocelyn went swiftly to obey, making do with a sketchy wash before re-doing her face and hair and slipping into her own evening clothes. A dash of perfume and she was ready. No one will look at me anyway, she thought as she sped down the servants' staircase to make her way round to the great hall where already the first arrivals were being shown to their seats.

Simon was standing at the foot of the grand staircase down which the models would walk to step straight on to the catwalk specially put up for the occasion. The flower-decked wrought iron banister rails curved and narrowed as they rose to the upper floor, making a perfect setting for the appearance of the girls now waiting upstairs to make their entrance.

The gilt chairs were full when a hush in the babble of conversation heralded the arrival of the Royal personage who was honouring the evening with her presence. Simon at once dispatched Jocelyn to warn his mother and by the time she returned to the hall the opening speech by the President of the charitable organization responsible for the function was ending and Simon stepped up to the microphone to make his first announcement.

A ripple of applause broke out before he finished speaking and Jocelyn looked up to see Candida at the head of the magnificent staircase, a vision of loveliness in shell pink nightdress and negligée embellished with ostrich feathers and with high-heeled satin slippers on her small feet. The ripple broke into a real burst of clapping as she reached the catwalk, pirouetted and then walked gracefully on as Simon's soft though penetrating tones described her attire.

As one creation after another was shown there was no doubt in Jocelyn's mind why Candida was at the top of her profession, for whether in a nightdress, hair tumbling about her shoulders, in a bikini looking like a little girl with hair bunched in ribbons, or svelte in day and evening clothes, she far outshone the other girls in both looks and technique. At the end of the parade when she appeared in the time-honoured bridal gown, the other girls in brides-maids' dresses of every colour with wide floppy hats, Jo-celyn unconsciously joined in the general gasp of admiration before all other sound was drowned by the applause. A glance at Simon's face showed that he too had his eyes fixed on the graceful figure in white now leading the others back up the stairs. At the top, Candida stopped, turned and posed to smile delightedly back on her admirers, and though Jocelyn knew this had not been rehearsed, it took the audience by storm, as no doubt Candida had intended.

Long after the last figure had disappeared, the ap-plause continued and it was several minutes before the audience rose and began to drift towards the supper room. Simon stuffed the last list into his pocket and turned, a satisfied smile on his lips. 'You must admit she has style,' he grinned. 'How about a drink to celebrate? I know I could do with one.'

Shaken by resentment at Simon's open admiration for Candida, Jocelyn hastily made her excuses. 'I can't leave your mother to cope alone.'

'Of course,' Simon frowned. 'I'd forgotten. See you later. Don't be too long,' he ordered as he strolled away.

Despite this admonitory reminder, an hour later Jo-celyn was still upstairs. The packers had removed the col-lections, the girls had changed to go and enjoy themselves with the crowd downstairs, and even Mrs. Wadebridge had disappeared, leaving Jocelyn to try and bring the rooms used by the girls into some semblance of order. She had just deposited a pile of used tissues, a pair of laddered tights and some false eyelashes she discovered coyly adhering to the rim of a washhand basin into a conveniently large wastepaper basket when the middle-aged housekeeper who had helped her recover the missing dress boxes came into the room.

'The staff will see to all this in the morning, miss. Please don't trouble yourself.'

'It was in a dreadful mess,' Jocelyn explained. 'I couldn't leave it looking so untidy.'

The housekeeper glanced round, then turned to smile. 'The maid will do the rest now. A nice young lady like you should be having a good time with the others, not playing Cinderella.'

Jocelyn smiled, a grateful light in her eyes. She discarded the jacket which matched her dress as Janey had suggested, tidied her hair and walked to the lower floor by way of the rear stairs. She reached the side hall just in time to see Pablo Pendleton and his assistant carrying their equipment to the exit door and asked, 'Not staying?'

Pablo grinned. 'Steve and I have just about every distinguished face in the place on film, so I reckon we can call it a day. I promised Angie I wouldn't stay late. She swears I shall get home one night to find a note pinned to the door reading "Gone to maternity hospital" and it will be all over.'

Jocelyn laughed as the outer door closed behind him and she tried to find someone she recognized among the sea of faces crowding the rooms and hallways, stopping when she came to where dancing was in progress. The orchestra was playing a haunting melody and across the room Jocelyn could just pick out Candida Melbourne in Simon's arms.

If she had looked beautiful in the gorgeous clothes she had modelled earlier she looked equally lovely now in a dress of lilac pink deepening in colour down the length of the skirt to a violet-shaded frill at the hemline. The material swirled softly with every movement and glancing around Jocelyn saw she wasn't the only one watching the pair on the fringe of the dance floor. Mrs. Wadebridge, a glass of wine in her hand, was talking to some people about ten feet away, but her eyes were anxiously watching her son and his partner.

As Jocelyn turned away a hand touched her arm and she discovered Walter Hook by her side. 'Where've you been? I've been looking for you everywhere,' he said without hesitation. 'Come on, let me get you some supper before everything runs out.'

The buffet was so lavish there was no danger of that. Walter, carrying two loaded plates, a bottle and two glasses, easily found them an unoccupied table, for though people were coming and going steadily the supper room was not crowded and they were able to converse with ease as they sampled the selection on their plates.

It must have been some twenty minutes later when Jocelyn was entertaining Walter with an anecdote which had occurred during the preparation for the show that she became aware of a silent third. Standing beside the table waiting only for a break in their conversation was Simon, and a glance of his expression was anything but reassuring.

He addressed his first remark, however, to Walter. 'Sorry to butt in, but I've been looking for Jocelyn. Has she told you our news?'

'News?' Walter looked taken aback as Simon announced bluntly,

'We're going to be married. I've arranged a bit of a party for the staff after work tomorrow to make an official announcement.'

Walter got slowly to his feet, holding out his hand to Simon. 'Congratulations, you're a lucky man.' Turning a reproachful look on Jocelyn herself, he added, 'The best

of luck, Jo, and all my good wishes for your happiness.'
He seemed to have lost his appetite, for after a few
minutes he made his excuses and slipped away. Jocelyn
watched his retreating back, wishing he had not looked so
hurt.

But a glance across the table at Simon's inscrutable face
showed her a much more pressing problem looming
nearby. Jocelyn was quick to recognize his moods and this
one usually preceded a reprimand for some oversight. He
could be singularly cutting when he chose, though to do
him justice, Simon never found fault with anyone in front
of an audience. He was scrupulously fair, waiting until he
had you alone to speak his mind and perhaps give you a
chance to frame an excuse.

The trouble was, Jocelyn thought as she felt her mouth
go dry, she never had the courage to do more than stand
and take whatever Simon chose to hand out, her tongue
twisting into knots at the first words of criticism. He was
watching her now between half closed eyes apparently
waiting for her to break the silence. As so often before she
could find no words. At last, apparently wishing to cut
short her obvious distress, Simon said gently, 'I thought
you and Walter were buddies.'

Jocelyn was surprised into instant response. 'We are.'

'Yet it didn't occur to you to tell him you'd agreed to
marry me? I should have got you a ring immediately to
seal the bargain. With your badge of office in place you
can't pretend you're not spoken for.'

The tone was decidedly humorous, but there was no
sign of amusement in Simon's face. Was he deliberately
punishing her or just keeping a poker face as he 'took the
mickey'? It was difficult to tell, and Jocelyn blushed
faintly, hoping that in the warm atmosphere of the
supper room Simon would think she was just over-
heated.

'Must I have a ring? You know how careless I am with
jewellery. Dad gave Mother's engagement ring to Janice

46

for that very reason. He said I'd have left it in some cloakroom the first time I washed my hands.'

To Jocelyn's surprise, Simon let out a shout of laughter and the deep laughter lines at the corners of his eyes crinkled as he took a small jeweller's box out of his pocket. 'You may lose this to your heart's content. If you do, I'll just have to buy another. But an engagement ring you're going to have, my girl, make no mistake about that. Do you like it? I've got it on approval, so we can change it for something else if you prefer.'

He opened the box as he spoke and Jocelyn let out a gasp of sheer pleasure. Somehow she hadn't expected Simon's choice would be anything like the unusual ring sparkling against the velvet lining. As she said nothing Simon stretched out a hand and slipped the ring on her third finger. It was shaped like a rose, with gold filigree petals and twelve small diamonds at its centre forming the stamen.

To her astonishment it was a perfect fit. 'How on earth did you guess the size?'

This time there was a little-boy conceit in the eyes now smiling beguilingly into hers. 'Clever of me, wasn't it? I stole one of your gloves. Now do you like it or shall we change it?'

Jocelyn, moving her hand to and fro to catch the light, said almost bemusedly, 'Change it? Of course not. It's lovely. But I'll be terrified to wear it,' she admitted.

'You'll have good reason to be even more terrified if you don't.' Simon's voice sounded remorseless. 'If you're so afraid of leaving it on a washbasin, wash with it on.'

Jocelyn sighed. Like most girls she had dreamed of that magic moment when having found the proverbial Mr. Right she had an engagement ring placed on her finger. In her imagination there had been moonlight, music and a nebulous man swearing undying love. True, there was music; the latest top of the hit parade was floating into the supper room. But Simon's words were anything but romantic and he was pocketing the little box as he got to his feet with something akin to relief in his eyes as if he had just brushed safely through a rather tricky business deal.

'If you've finished supper I suggest we mingle. I know Mother wants a word now the show is successfully behind her and she can relax.'

Jocelyn allowed Simon to guide her to Betty Wade-bridge's side, obediently displayed the engagement ring at his signal and was rewarded by a swift hug from her future mother-in-law. 'I'm so relieved he's chosen you.'

It was hardly a reassuring comment and for once Jocelyn was not sorry to leave Mrs. Wadebridge when Simon suggested the music was too good to be wasted. As they circled the floor the scene held an element of unreality which even the beautiful ring on her finger could not dispel.

When the music ceased they were standing beside Candida Melbourne and her partner, a tall foreign-looking man in his early thirties. Candida introduced him and a few minutes later Jocelyn found herself dancing with the attractive Frenchman, though how the change over had come about she could not have said. But if Jocelyn was frequently reduced to silence when in Simon's company she felt little shyness with others. By the time the waltz ended she and Philippe Vernay were the best of friends and he was laughing delightedly at Jocelyn's attempts to talk to him in his own language.

Perhaps it was the admiration she glimpsed in her partner's eyes, maybe the ring on her finger gave her confidence, but suddenly Jocelyn felt lighthearted. If Simon was going to make a habit of deserting her, he wasn't going to return and find her languishing like a wallflower. She was laughing up into Philippe's face as he whispered a compliment into her ear when Simon and Candida reappeared. There was a sulky look about the beautiful lips as Candida announced, 'I'm thirsty. Let's have some champagne,' and slipping her arm through Philippe's she pulled him away before he had time to give only a Gallic shrug of apology.

'Methinks our friend was somewhat reluctant to leave.' Simon was standing behind her chair, so Jocelyn could only guess at his expression, but the tone of voice encouraged her by its faint note of pique.

'Yes, I think he was. Candida can be a bit imperious.'

'You could call it that,' to Jocelyn's surprise Simon actually chuckled, 'or you could say she was as subtle as a meat axe. She just doesn't like competition. Still, what are we doing discussing Candida and missing the chance to dance to this music? I like this tune.'

He pulled Jocelyn on to the floor and into his arms, holding her much more closely than before. This was more like it, Jocelyn thought, closing her eyes. It only needed a pinch of imagination to get carried away, fancy this really was the happiest day of her life instead of a purely business arrangement. When the music stopped she opened her eyes to find Simon watching her. 'Tired? I guess you are at that. Come on, let's collect Mother and Candida and head for home.'

But it transpired that Candida had other plans. A more attractive offer had come her way and she had agreed to join a party bent on dancing the night away. Simon collected his mother and when the car was brought to the door Mrs. Wadebridge immediately got into the back, declaring that all she wanted to do was kick her shoes off and doze all the way back to London. 'Wake me when we're home,' she requested as Simon engaged the gears.

Once the journey had begun Simon seemed disinclined to talk. He kept his eyes on the road ahead and as the silence lengthened Jocelyn stole a glance at his profile. It was anything but reassuring, the lips in a tight line, she saw as another car, its headlights full on, came towards them. Eventually, lulled by the quiet hum of the engine, Jocelyn herself fell asleep, awakening only when Simon pulled up outside her door, and she found that some time during the drive, despite the restriction of a seat belt, she had slipped sideways on the well upholstered seat, for her head lay against Simon's arm.

She sat upright and unashamedly rubbed her eyes. 'Sorry! I seem to have used you as a pillow.'

Simon stopped in the act of opening the driver's door to turn his head. In the dim overhead light he seemed to be smiling. 'My pleasure,' then he was out of the car and coming round to help her out. She was aware of a vague disappointment at his prosaic 'See you tomorrow.' He might at least have kissed her cheek.

It did not take Jocelyn long next morning to discover that news of the engagement was all round the agency and regarded as something of a nine days' wonder. Indeed the surprise shown by one or two of the permanent staff was unflatteringly frank. It was something of an ordeal therefore to stand later that evening and hear Simon make the official announcement of his mother's resignation and their forthcoming marriage. As the staff politely toasted the occasion Jocelyn pretended not to notice curiosity in more than one pair of eyes.

It was Gwenda who called out, 'Aren't you going to kiss the bride-to-be?' and as Jocelyn's eyes turned in mute appeal Simon put down his glass to give her a derisive smile. She felt sick, breathless and faint all at the same time as his arms encircled her, and was only prevented from active resistance at his whispered, 'Relax! They're all watching.'

The kiss was over so quickly that for a moment Jocelyn blinked at the cheers of approval, then smiled shakily as she again met Simon's eyes and the unspoken command she read there.

She was thankful when people drifted away to go home for the night, for her face felt as if it were aching from the bright smile she had kept resolutely in place.

But the day's ordeals were not over yet. She was locking her desk when Mrs. Wadebridge came in. 'Come and have supper at our place, Jocelyn. There's a lot to discuss and never enough time here. Simon's ready, so we can get away now.' Sitting in growing indignation at the dining-table, however, for all the attention paid to her opinions, Jocelyn felt she might just as well have gone home. The reorganization at the agency, plans for their wedding and honeymoon, the date of Mrs. Wadebridge's departure for her own wedding in America, were argued out between Simon and his mother as if Jocelyn were invisible.

As she ate mouthfuls of feather-light lemon mousse she pondered on the possible reaction were she suddenly to open her mouth and veto just one of the propositions. No doubt they would be as surprised as if a pet cat had turned and bitten them. Even acute Simon, catching the self-pitying smile curving her lips, did not seem to sense her humiliation at being ignored. At his, 'Anything the matter?' Jocelyn shook her head.

'You wouldn't understand,' she said, then turned immediately to ask Mrs. Wadebridge, 'Shall I fetch the coffee?'

'Would you? I told Mrs. Telford to go as soon as we got home, but I expect she'll have left a tray ready.' When Jocelyn returned Simon and Mrs. Wadebridge had moved to the living-room and Simon was pouring brandy into three glasses. 'I know you don't usually indulge, Mother, but it will do you good. You look tired. You too, Jocelyn.'

Jocelyn poured coffee into the three small cups, then added sugar and poured the measure of brandy into her own coffee. She looked up to meet Simon's amused glance. 'The spirit should go in first.'

'I like it this way,' Jocelyn retorted defiantly, then blushed when his smile grew as if her small rebellion amused him. Had he perhaps been aware of her mutinous feelings during the last hour? Recognized the inclination to scream her objections at the plans being made over her head?

Old habits die hard, however, and Jocelyn kept silent, just as she kept silent when Simon took her home later, this time to kiss her good night in the approved manner. 'I'm sorry our trial run was in full view of the public eye,' he remarked as his lips left hers. 'You'll have to get used to this from now on.'

'Meaning kissing me from time to time?' Jocelyn asked, wishing he would hurry up and leave.

'You might even get to like it,' he answered cruelly, watching her flush as he took the key out of her hand. 'Off to bed now, and don't stay up gossiping with Janey,' he ordered, opening the door and pushing her gently inside.

But there was no Janey to chat with even had she been in the mood, only a note saying 'Doing stand-in night duty. See you eight a.m.,' propped against the kettle. Jocelyn made herself a hot drink and got ready for bed. At breakfast tomorrow she would have to tell Janey the wedding was on despite her plea for reprieve.

On the morning of her wedding day Jocelyn still felt bemused as if the last three weeks filled with preparations for her wedding and the rearrangement of the staff in anticipation of Mrs. Wadebridge's retirement had been done by someone with no relation to herself. All the arguments with Janey, her family's candid surprise at her engagement to Simon were behind. Today, for better or worse, she was committed to becoming Mrs. Simon Wadebridge.

Now at last reality was breaking through the layers of detachment with which she had protected herself, and a feeling of near panic made her get up and walk to the window. The gardens in front of the block of flats were gay with tulips and wallflowers while in the distance the tops of the tall trees in the park could be seen, the pale green of their new leaves showing clearly over the roofs of the houses opposite. Jocelyn had a sudden impulse to run

away, tear off the elaborate wedding outfit Mrs. Wadebridge had chosen, climb into jeans and pullover and
escape from an impossible situation. But her father was in
the living-room waiting for the car to come back after
taking Margaret and Janey to the church and in half an
hour or so she would be swearing away the only inde-
pendence Simon Wadebridge had left her.

Always at the back of her mind was the thought of her
young brother. She had written and asked him to come to
the wedding, but there had been no reply. What Simon
said to him the day he handed over the money to pay
Alan's gambling debt she never discovered, but it had
certainly made her brother retire behind a curtain of
silence.

In the big hired car, her feeling of isolation increased so
that she was only dimly aware of her father's intermittent
attempts at conversation. What would Janey have said
had she asked her for a tranquillizer? Jocelyn wondered —
not that there was any need, for she felt half anaesthetized,
as if an automaton had taken her place. But the temporary insensitivity had not dulled her powers of obser-
vation; Jocelyn was keenly aware of Janey's anxious
glance as she straightened her veil before she began the
walk up the long aisle to where Simon awaited her and
felt momentary surprise at the number of people who had
gathered to watch this odd and obviously unexpected
union.

As well as a sprinkling of relatives from both families,
practically the entire staff of Wadebridge's appeared to be
crowded into the front pews. Only Walter Hook sat con-
spicuously alone and Jocelyn deliberately looked away as
he turned to watch her approach.

The ceremony itself passed like a waking dream right
until the moment when Simon slid the slim gold band on
to her finger and repeated the clergyman's words. A cold
shiver went down Jocelyn's spine, but if Simon felt the
uncontrollable shudder he gave no sign, and glancing at

his intent face, Jocelyn saw clearly that he looked somehow different. His eyes were on the hand he held between his own as he echoed the time-honoured 'With this ring ...' and when they knelt for the blessing he possessed himself quite naturally of Jocelyn's other hand and the warmth flowing from his fingers into her own icy cold ones served to check the tide of rising hysteria.

By the time the register was completed Jocelyn had regained her usual composure, and if she looked paler than normal as she signed her maiden name for the last time no one was unkind enough to remark on the fact.

The reception afterwards held all the accustomed ordeals for both bride and groom, the over-demonstrative declarations of good luck and kisses of congratulations, the risqué jokes, nothing, Jocelyn thought, a polite smile curving her lips, seemed to have been spared them. She was astonished to feel relief as the time came for them to leave, despite more well-meaning but none the less embarrassing remarks as someone spotted Simon's golf clubs in the back of the car, for to Jocelyn's secret astonishment he had booked them into a quiet country hotel on the borders of Dorset and Devon.

They had been on the road for about an hour before Simon did more than ask if she were comfortable or wanted the window open, then he surprised her by asking quietly, 'Why are you so scared of me? I've often wondered.'

Jocelyn, who had been watching the countryside flash past her window, almost panicked into a denial, but without taking his eyes from the road ahead Simon continued, 'Please don't lie and deny it. I've seen a look of apprehension on your face too often to be mistaken.' He glanced swiftly at her and away again. 'You've got it now, as a matter of fact. As if you were afraid I was going to gobble you up in one mouthful.'

Jocelyn moistened her lips and decided on the simple truth. 'I can't give you an honest answer, for I don't know myself.' She stopped then as Simon was patiently waiting for her to enlarge on her statement she said half apologetically, 'I guess it's because you always make me feel inadequate. I've never been able to understand why you kept me on as a secretary, let alone asked me to marry you. Why did you, Simon? Was it because I conveniently know your ways, and I'm the sort of girl who will fade into the background and cause you no embarrassment?'

It was a courageous question for Jocelyn and she even wondered at her own temerity in saying out loud what had been nagging at her ever since Simon proposed. She fell silent, watching Simon surreptitiously out of the corner of her eye. It was something of an anti-climax when he actually answered. 'What a man-sized inferiority complex you've got, kitten! What started it? Middle child syndrome? I know your mother and father doted on Janice and spoiled Alan because he was the youngest as well as the only boy, but what makes you think you're so inefficient as a secretary and nondescript as a person? You say you know my ways. If that's so, when have you known me tolerate a bad employee for one single instant? Even without the personal aspect involved, had you not been more than on top of your job right from the start you'd have been out on your ear. All you needed was a guiding hand when it came to clothes and make-up. Have you hated that too? Been made to feel you're incapable of choosing wisely? If you have, just get out a snapshot of yourself five years ago and take a good look at it. You won't be able to tell it's the same girl. You used to come to work looking like a gipsy, and an unattractive one at that. You, with all your possibilities and potential!'

Jocelyn flashed Simon a look of amazement. In all the years she had known him she had never before heard Simon Wadebridge favour her with an explanation of his opinions, and this was certainly a lengthy one. But during it he had left unanswered the second part of her question, his reason for choosing her as his bride. Had the elaborate analysis of her psychological reflexes been merely to take her attention away from the one inquiry he hadn't chosen to clarify? It had not succeeded in satisfying her curiosity, but Jocelyn lacked the courage to ask again. She sighed as she turned her head away, both for her own lack of bravery and for the knowledge that Simon could subtly twist her any way he wanted. It must be nice to have this power to mould others to any pattern you desired, she mused, as the powerful car carried them swiftly towards their destination.

CHAPTER THREE

THE hotel was a good deal larger than Jocelyn had anticipated and must at one time, she imagined, have been
someone's country home before staffing difficulties made
it a white elephant. As soon as Simon braked in front of
the stone steps leading to a glassed-in porch, a uniformed
porter came to collect their baggage while another
slipped into Simon's seat to garage the car.

The large entrance hall was quiet, most of the other
guests apparently changing before dinner, though
through the doorway near the reception desk Jocelyn noticed a sprinkling of people talking over drinks in a cosy
cocktail bar. The service was quiet, efficient, discreet, and
soon Simon was guiding Jocelyn along a thickly carpeted
corridor to where the porter was waiting beside an open
door.

It led into one of the most enormous bedrooms Jocelyn
had ever seen, with a bay window overlooking the rear
gardens and the private golf course beyond. Behind the
golf course wooded hills rose in the distance, and as Jocelyn, drawn to the view, leaned out the scent from
flowers in the herbaceous borders below rose strongly on
the evening breeze.

Stepping back, she discovered Simon watching her
with his head a little to one side and a distinct twinkle in
his grey eyes. 'I take it you approve of the place?'

'Oh yes, it's beautiful. How did you come to find it? I
never heard you mention this part of the country.'

Simon laughed. 'You may have been my personal secretary for five years, but you don't know all my secrets! I
used to come down here sometimes for a quiet week-end
when the agency got on top of me.'

Jocelyn's eyes widened. Simon was right when he disputed her claim of knowing all his ways, for it was certainly an eye-opener to be told that he had never been oppressed by business responsibilities. If asked to give an opinion she would have said Simon found running the agency a challenge he enjoyed despite its problems, financial or otherwise. It was certainly more than surprising to discover he had sometimes felt the need to escape for a few days of peace and quiet.

'Do you want to wash first, or shall we unpack?' Jocelyn was jogged out of her abstraction by Simon's question.

'You use the bathroom. I'll unpack for both of us,' she offered, while the unwelcome misgivings popped through her mind that Simon seemed so much at ease this was probably not the first time he had shared a double room with a girl. But as she opened the cases and began to hang their clothes in the fitted wardrobe Jocelyn firmly dismissed these unwelcome thoughts. What was past was past and Simon's distractions when single were not any of her business.

Jocelyn woke with a start the following morning as a knock on the door roused her out of a deep sleep. Simon, a towel draped casually round his middle and with his hair still wet from the shower, came out of the bathroom saying, 'Lie still. I'll get it,' returning a few minutes later to put a tray of morning tea on the bedside table and add, 'Don't wait for me. I'll finish shaving, then you can have your bath.'

She sat up slowly and poured out a cup of the steaming liquid. It was certainly a novelty to awake to the company of a half-naked man in one's room, and not an unpleasant novelty at that. It was years since she had seen Simon in anything but formal attire and she had forgotten his well-proportioned physique. He had tanned easily as a boy and this morning his skin against the stark white of his bath towel had been brown and healthy-looking. Jocelyn picked up her tea cup and snuggling into the nest of pillows let her eyes gaze dreamily out at the sunshine.

So far the married state had proved a good deal more congenial than she could ever have anticipated, and for this, Jocelyn knew, she had Simon to thank. For a man who made no protestations or avowals of undying love he had certainly behaved in an unexpectedly gentle and tender fashion. His had been the diplomacy and ease of manner which had killed her inner fears at birth, for she had never expected to awake today feeling at peace with the world and ready to face eventualities. Simon Wadebridge might have made a marriage convenient to his needs, but he obviously did not intend his bride to have complaints that he did not give her all the attention of a normal, newly-wedded husband.

She was jolted out of her reverie by Simon vacating the bathroom, now conventionally dressed and with every hair in place. He sat beside her on the bed, poured his own tea and said, 'I thought we'd breakfast as soon as you're dressed, Kitten, then perhaps you'd like to walk round the course with me. Got some flat-heeled shoes with you?' Jocelyn nodded. 'I know you don't play golf, but it's a lovely day, the fresh air will do you good. Anyway, I don't want to let you out of my sight.'

He might almost mean it, he sounded so plausible, Jocelyn thought as she showered and dressed in the well-appointed bathroom adjoining their bedroom, but common sense intervened. She had heard Simon convincing doubtful clients and temperamental employees too often not to know he had a talent for pulling the wool over people's eyes if he thought circumstances merited it.

During the days that followed, however, he continued to turn what for Jocelyn had loomed as a period to be got through as best she could into a round of companionable and uninterrupted pleasure hitherto not experienced in her busy life. Every morning she accompanied him round the golf course, sometimes to Simon's evident amusement trying a shot with an old ball, and after lunch they explored the neighbourhood. In the evening they ate alone in a corner of the hushed candlelit dining-room and at night she slept in his arms, for Simon had not been joking when he said he did not intend to let her out of his sight.

There was something to be said for having an attractive husband, Jocelyn thought as they went in to dinner on the last day of their short honeymoon and she caught the half inviting glance a sparkling brunette cast at Simon as he followed close behind her. The dark-haired girl in the stunning evening dress was still staring across at their table when the waiter spread the dazzling white napkin across Jocelyn's lap and handed her the menu.

'What do you fancy tonight, Kitten?' Simon was studying his own menu and seemed completely unaware of the interest he had aroused. As they chose their meal Jocelyn watched him, envying his self-confidence and sangfroid until catching her eye, Simon grinned and asked, 'What now? You're looking at me exactly like a small cat who wonders if she's about to be shut out for the night.'

'Is that why you call me Kitten?' Jocelyn asked, ignoring the question and womanlike answering by asking one of her own.

Simon's lips curled up at the corners a little more as he reached across and took her hand. 'Just a pet name which suits you. Tell me, have you enjoyed the last few days? You do realize it's been a chance to get to know one another better which we shan't have time for once Mother departs?' He released her to lean back and Jocelyn suddenly realized his mind had already returned to grapple with the agency's problems, for he frowned and went on, 'It will take some time for Gwenda to become anything like as good as you, and Walter will never sit in my seat, wizard though he is with a set of ledgers. You'll soon be coping with Mother's side of the business as efficiently as she has always done, but what happens when we both want to get away together? It will need some thought.'

He evidently began to do just this, for he was markedly silent during the first half of the meal as he ate his way through a portion of smoked salmon followed by half a duckling. But Simon was as hard on himself as he frequently was with others, and Jocelyn observed that he made a marked effort to throw off the problems perplexing him to make an attempt to keep a conversation going. In a way it saddened her that he thought it necessary to put on an act, appear as though he had nothing on his mind apart from the enjoyment of the last night of their holiday.

Jocelyn had begun to think during the last days that she and Simon had reached some sort of rapport and his words a few moments ago had made her imagine he felt the same. But as the meal continued it was apparent that Simon was not so full of joie de vivre as he was pretending, and it hurt that he still thought it necessary to be entertaining, as if she were no more than a casual acquaintance he was wining and dining.

Would she ever understand this enigmatic man she had married? Jocelyn wondered when the waiter placed the coffee tray on the table. The intimacy of marriage seemed to have done nothing to break down the barrier of reserve behind which he frequently retreated. There was only one cause for congratulation. At least if Simon was concerned about who would take over the running of Wadebridge's during their absence he had not married her to get a built-in manageress so that he could go away alone whenever the mood took him.

But if Simon could play his cards close to his chest so could she, Jocelyn decided, and tonight had given her a pointer on how to behave when they returned to London and the public eye. She had almost begun to soften, feel perhaps she had misjudged him, but Simon's habit of keeping things to himself continued to rankle. If he was going to issue orders, make decisions and ignore her wish to be a real help perhaps become privy to his intentions, so be it. She too could put on an act, build an armour of indifference around herself, for Jocelyn suspected that she wasn't as unresponsive to Simon's particular brand of masculine charm as she had been five days ago. He had been gentle, tender and patient, displaying a side to his character she had not dreamed existed, and Jocelyn knew she could now be hurt where once his apparent ruthlessness had only made her shake with inner fear and frustrated anger.

It felt strange to walk into the office and find Anne and a stranger in the outer office and see Gwenda sitting behind her old familiar desk. No more would she have Simon issuing orders through the intercom, for until she left for America she would share Mrs. Wadebridge's office. Here prospective clients who preferred a reputable firm like Wadebridge's to handle their appointments could be interviewed and would-be student models attempting to get vacancies on the crowded course could be weeded out.

They came in all ages, sizes and types, for Wadebridge's motto was that they could supply models for all needs, from a baby for nappy advertisements to someone to promote a cure for asthma.

Thes days which followed were busy and for Jocelyn held some surprises. During their absence a farewell party for Mrs. Wadebridge had been arranged, and Gwenda, showing a flair for organization hitherto unsuspected, had kept it a secret until the last minute not only from Mrs, Wadebridge herself but from Simon and Jocelyn as well. Following Mrs. Wadebridge's departure Jocelyn began to sense a subtle alteration in the attitude of people towards her. She concluded wryly that evidently Mrs. Simon

Wadebridge was considered more important and influential that Miss Jocelyn Ashtead had been and worth cultivating in consequence. She had always enjoyed a pleasant relationship with clients and fellow members of the staff, but it was surprising how many who had formerly treated her only with detached politeness now frequently hailed her in a much more intimate manner.

Jocelyn was level-headed enough to take this change of climate with a liberal pinch of salt, ignoring the compliments and flattery as something of no real importance which she would have to learn to live with. More difficult was her life outside the office, for after her mother-in-law's departure the flat seemed very empty without Betty Wadebridge's cheerful personality to smooth away the awkward moments and whose matter of fact manner Jocelyn found infinitely soothing.

Sometimes Simon retired to his study to work after their evening meal, and when she was left alone to watch T.V. or sew the close relationship of the first few days of her marriage seemed a million miles away. Their bedroom contained twin beds and often Jocelyn, bored with her own company, had been in bed some time before she heard Simon tiptoe in to get undressed. His dedication to the continued success of the agency was little excuse, she thought bitterly, for withdrawal of the attention she had enjoyed during the brief honeymoon. The only chink in the dreary pattern of bed and work had been Angie Pendleton's heart-warming invitation for Jocelyn to stand godmother to her new baby son.

Despite Jocelyn's feelings of vague dissatisfaction days, then weeks slipped by. Simon, an early riser, was usually first up to make the early morning tea. While Jocelyn prepared breakfast he showered and shaved, for Mrs. Telford, who had her own key, did not come until mid-morning. The rest of the day Jocelyn was too busy in the office to consider the disadvantages or otherwise of her altered circumstances and once or twice a week they entertained business guests at the flat or dined out with friends.

One day towards the end of June, Simon brought a stranger into Jocelyn's office. 'Meet Neville Newton, Jocelyn. He's going to join the firm.' Simon's voice held a cautionary note and Jocelyn, looking up to smile politely and extend her hand, was careful not even to look the question she was longing to ask. Who was the swarthily handsome man shaking her by the hand, and what was to be his function? Simon's mother would not have been kept in the dark until the last moment like this, Jocelyn thought rebelliously, and behind the newcomer's back she threw an expressive glance in Simon's direction.

He smiled sardonically at her disapproval and turned away, saying, 'I'll show you over the rest of the place before lunch, but I wanted you first of all to meet my wife. You'll be working quite a bit with her,' and his smile mocked as the two men went away. Jocelyn sat trying to cool her anger, only to discover that unpalatable shocks were not over for the day. As they were about to leave, Simon burst his second bombshell.

'By the way, we're having a house guest for a bit. With having Newton around all day I quite forgot to mention it. When Pablo was up north last week he saw a girl he thinks will be ideal for that gravy advertisement he's got scheduled for the autumn. You may remember him mentioning it. The idea is to promote it as a product fitted for any environment, be it castle or Girl Guide camp, and the whole campaign revolves on a plan to use the same girl. Everyone I suggested Pablo turned down. He doesn't want a run-of-the-mill model but someone a bit out of the ordinary who won't look out of place whether wearing a uniform or ermine cloak and coronet. He thinks he's found the very girl, spotted her in a shop in Newcastle, I believe. He's already done a couple of pilot shots and he says Patricia has a great future. But she knows nothing about make-up or camera technique and he wants us to rough off the loose corners. The trouble is, she knows no one in London and Angie has been putting her up for a couple of days. With the baby there now it's a bit difficult. I told Pablo as Mother's room's going to waste we'd take over until the girl can find a place of her own. You might arrange elocution lessons for her too.'

This last remark temporarily diverted Jocelyn's thoughts. 'What for? Even for a T.V. commercial she won't necessarily have to speak. They nearly always dub the voices.'

'Just the same, it wouldn't hurt to tone her regional accent down a trifle. It's a bit difficult to understand her at times.'

Jocelyn closed her lips on her more pressing objections and asked in a tight voice, 'Am I to understand she's already installed?' to which Simon replied, 'Of course. I thought you'd welcome a female house guest. You've given me the impression lately that you miss having no other woman around. Possibly it's a bit lonely for you without Mother and Janey. I fully realize I'll never come up to their standards as a substitute.'

Jocelyn shot him a quick look, for if she hadn't known him better she might have suspected a note of regret in his deep voice. But it could hardly have been a hint of pique. Where there was no love there could be no hurt.

Mrs. Telford had the evening meal ready to serve when they reached the flat and when Jocelyn went into the kitchen she said, 'I've put the young lady in Mrs. Wadebridge's room. I hope she's all right, for she's not made a sound for the past hour.' On her way to freshen up, Jocelyn noticed that the door to their guest's room was closed, but the whereabouts of her unexpected visitor was soon discovered, for the bathroom door proved to be locked.

Jocelyn returned to the big living-room where Simon was pouring himself a drink to say tersely, 'Our guest seems to have taken root in the bathroom. I suppose you wouldn't like to tell her dinner is ready and Mrs. Telford is waiting to serve it before she leaves for the day?'

Simon looked up, caught the suppressed indignation in Jocelyn's eyes and laughed unexpectedly. 'Keep your hair on, Kitten! Come and have a drink and relax. Mrs. Telford's been here too long to give notice for such a trivial matter as an unpunctual guest, so stop worrying.'

Reluctantly Jocelyn smiled and went to join him, choosing an iced Dubonnet and bitter lemon to cool her temper. They had finished their drinks and even Simon was beginning to glance at his watch when at last Patricia Winningford appeared in the doorway.

Jocelyn didn't know quite what she had expected, but this girl fitted into no category she had ever seen before in all her years at the agency. Hair a mousy brown, badly in need of styling, she also had an unfashionably wide mouth with not even an outstanding figure to catch the eye, and as they sat down to the meal Mrs. Telford had put out in the dining alcove at one end of the big L-shaped room, Jocelyn could not help marvelling at Pablo Pendleton's enthusiasm. But as the meal progressed Jocelyn noticed that Simon appeared as impressed as Pablo by this unknown girl's potential. Furthermore, he seemed to experience no difficulty in fathoming out the marked north-country accent and he carried on a non-stop conversation in which Jocelyn was odd man out.

She was not sorry when the time came to clear away and make coffee for Mrs. Telford had long gone. When she returned with a loaded tray it was to hear Simon say, 'We shall have to think of another name for you, of course. Patricia Winningford's much too long. One name only these days is best, of course. Who can forget names like Lulu or Twiggy? Any suggestions?'

The next twenty minutes were spent trying and discarding innumerable suggestions. Patricia's favourite was Samantha, but Simon disapproved on the grounds that it made her sound like a new model of doll. His own more

66

unusual exotic recommendations Patricia herself declined on the grounds that she didn't look like an Elfreda, an Amaryllis or a Rosetta.

'What were you called at school?' Simon asked at last in desperation, and when Patricia answered 'Paddy' wrinkled his nose in disgust. 'We must come up with something,' he remarked, going across to pour himself a brandy, then he turned sharply as Jocelyn, who had taken no part in the recent discussion, said quietly, 'Why don't you call yourself simply "Padwyn" spelled with a Y instead of an I? It's a combination of your names and the sort of pseudonym people might remember.'

'By Jove, Kitten, I believe you've got it!' Simon said, apparently unconscious of how nearly he had parodied a popular song. 'What do you think, Patricia? Would Padwyn as a professional label suit you?'

Patricia certainly did not display as much enthusiasm for her new name as Simon, but by bedtime it was agreed that this should be used for publicity purposes. Jocelyn by the time she prepared for bed had received the distinct impression that Patricia Winningford was the sort of girl who would have welcomed the idea a good deal more had it originated from Simon's brain instead of her own.

Indeed in the days that followed, as she steered the agency's newest recruit through the intricacies of her crash course, it became glaringly obvious that 'Padwyn' had little or no time for her own sex and only came to life when a man was around. She switched on like an electric light every time a member of the opposite sex hove in sight, and even shy Walter Hook admitted to Jocelyn over coffee in her office a week after Padwyn's arrival that he thought she'd 'go far'.

Jocelyn rather agreed. Though Padwyn wasn't her cup of tea Pablo had rarely been wrong in his assessment of a model's potential and could possibly have hit the jackpot again. This hitherto unknown girl might well make headlines, for despite her unspectacular looks she had the secret of projecting her personality on film so that she seemed to reach out to the viewer.

Jocelyn had been over to see Pablo's pilot pictures, and even without the gloss now being applied that unknown quantity known as charisma was very apparent. Once she learned the ropes Padwyn would probably have a huge success.

Travelling out to visit her father and stepmother one evening, Jocelyn realized she had seen very little of Simon for days and then rarely alone. During office hours training Neville Newton in the business he was fully occupied and in the evenings a conversation between herself, Simon and Padwyn usually ended in Jocelyn leaving the others to carry the burden of the discussion. It was almost a relief to have a good excuse to escape the ordeal of the evening meal tonight, although it had not done Jocelyn's ego much good when Simon, on hearing of her plans, announced, 'In that case I'll take Padwyn to the theatre. She says she's never seen Shakespeare performed by first class actors, and they're doing *The Taming of the Shrew* at the Old Vic.'

Jocelyn frequently wondered whether Padwyn had made any real attempt to find herself a place to live. If she didn't offer to move out soon, Jocelyn determined to speak to Simon, suggest he use his influence to get her a flatlet with bath and kitchen in one of the new blocks being built nearby and allow them once more the freedom of their own home.

For it was home no longer, Jocelyn thought with uncharacteristic resentment. Even evenings alone with Simon shut away in his study were preferable to being treated almost as an intruder in her own apartment. Padwyn always seemed to be in the bathroom when Jocelyn wanted to take her daily shower, she invited people in for drinks without so much as a 'by your leave' and had taken to monopolizing Mrs. Telford's time. The breaking point came the evening they were invited to the launching of a new product by one of the leading American cosmetic firms. Jocelyn discovered her own evening dress still hanging unpressed in the wardrobe while a flustered Mrs. Telford apologized on the grounds that, 'Miss Padwyn said you wouldn't mind doing your own as it's important hers is perfect.'

No wonder Angie Pendleton had made the new baby and lack of space an excuse to get rid of her husband's latest protégée! When she thanked Jocelyn for taking Padwyn off her hands she had added, 'I never imagined Simon would offer her accommodation so soon after your wedding. Still, it shouldn't be for long.' At the other end of the phone Jocelyn pulled a face, glad that Angie didn't suspect her marriage was not all it appeared, for in front of others Simon was usually conventionally affectionate.

It was a pleasant change, therefore, to go where one's welcome was a foregone conclusion. 'Pity Simon couldn't come as well,' Jack Ashtead said as they sat down to supper, and Jocelyn felt guilty at hiding the fact that she had never even contemplated the inclusion of Simon in her plan. Would he have come? she wondered. Or did an evening at the theatre with Padwyn appear to him a more agreeable way of ending a busy day? Since she hadn't the courage to ask she would never know, she mused as she helped herself to vegetables and began to entertain her father with an incident she knew would amuse him.

It was past eleven when she arrived home, but there was no sign of the others and the illuminated hands of Jocelyn's bedside clock pointed to one o'clock before she heard Simon's key in the door. Jocelyn closed her eyes and pretended to be asleep, but a determination to put an end to Padwyn's stay took root.

An opportunity to put her plan into operation came out of the blue the following day. A dozen students were coming for interview and Simon had suggested that Neville Newton sat in to see for himself exactly what qualities Jocelyn looked for in prospective models. They were having a break and discussing the merits of the six girls they had already interviewed when Neville suddenly asked, 'Has Padwyn found herself a place yet?'

Jocelyn glanced at him in surprise, but he was stirring his coffee and not looking in her direction. 'Not that I know of, she's far too comfortable with us.'

Despite her intention of sounding unconcerned Jocelyn knew a note of definite resentment had sounded in her reply, and Neville smiled broadly. 'I thought you looked a bit desperate. Think Padwyn would consider a vacancy in our flat? I've been sharing with my young student brother and a girl who's been on his course. She's leaving next week, so her room is going begging. Would Padwyn be interested, do you suppose?'

'I've really no idea,' Jocelyn smiled back, 'but if you're looking for someone who'll iron your shirts and do the cooking, think again. You'd be backing a non-starter!'

Neville crossed one elegantly clad leg over the other. 'Like that, is she? Still, the pleasure of her company would more than compensate for lack of the domestic skills.'

'You too?' Jocelyn asked before she could stop the words from popping out. She blushed faintly at the sympathy on Neville's face. 'Sorry, did that sound dog-in-the-mangerish?' she apologized hastily. 'It's just that everyone seems to think Padwyn is God's gift to the advertising world.'

'And you tend to get a bit uptight? Right? Neville finished for her. Jocelyn smiled shyly as she nodded, but Neville consoled her with, 'Don't feel guilty. I've met Padwyn's sort before. They have so much sex appeal they tend to bring out the worst in other women.'

As consolation it was a pretty poor effort, Jocelyn thought, but she forced herself to smile with as much warmth as she could muster and say, 'I'll mention your offer to Padwyn if you like,' to which Neville replied quickly, 'No, leave it to me.'

He must have proved singularly persuasive, for at supper that evening Padwyn announced that she would be moving out by the end of the week. 'Where to?' Simon inquired sharply. 'You don't want to be too far out, and some places right in town can prove pretty expensive. You've not made your fortune yet, remember.'

Padwyn smiled beguilingly into his eyes, ignoring Jocelyn watching from the other side of the table. 'Don't worry, this isn't expensive and it's very central. I've arranged to share with Neville and his brother.'

'I see.' Simon sounded dangerously quiet. 'Whose idea was this?' and he looked across at Jocelyn, who managed to return Simon's glance with one of bland innocence.

'Neville's, of course.' Padwyn sounded puzzled. 'You don't mind, do you, Simon?'

Simon switched his gaze back to the questioner. 'Of course I don't mind. I just hope you'll be comfortable, that's all.'

But later, when Jocelyn was reading in bed, Simon suddenly asked, 'Did you know Neville intended asking Padwyn to share?'

'He told me this morning. It's a perfect solution, for Neville's place isn't too far away, and Padwyn will be in her element with two men instead of just one at her beck and call.'

A deathly silence greeted this remark and Jocelyn looked up from her book to meet a pair of steely grey eyes. As she gazed nervously back, wondering what was coming, the ice faded and to her surprise Simon suddenly stopped what he was doing to come and perch on the edge of her bed. He took the book from her unresisting fingers and asked softly and caressingly, 'Been feeling left out in the cold, have you, Kitten? No need. Any attentions I pay to Padwyn are just in the line of business, so there's no real cause to feel jealous,' and he kissed first her soft

71

mouth, then, bending his head, the hollow of her shoulder.

Jocelyn's heart had begun to pound suffocatingly in the way it always did the moment Simon touched her, but several weeks of marriage had made her wary of revealing her reactions. As she gazed down at the top of Simon's head the unwelcome thought popped into her mind that perhaps this was always his inevitable method of smoothing away doubts, and not necessarily solely those of his wife. Was the philosophy a kind word and a kiss offered at the right moment the principle on which he based his actions? If this were true she could never trust Simon completely or feel at peace with him. But was it possible for any man to pretend so well? Behave with such apparent sincerity just to get his own way with the least inconvenience?

At this precise moment Simon looked up and caught her glance. He stroked the hair back from Jocelyn's forehead with a gentle hand. 'What's the matter, Kitten? You look defeated and as if things have got on top of you a bit. You've been doing too much since Mother left. Give Neville more of your work to handle. After all, that's why I persuaded him to join the firm.'

'Is it? I wondered exactly what his role was supposed to be.'

Simon sat back, his face expressionless. He studied Jocelyn for a moment in silence, then said, 'I thought you realized I want him to be able to stand in for both of us in time, but right now I'd like him to take some of the work load off your shoulders.'

Jocelyn lay back, tried to give Simon credit for sincere consideration and failed. 'You never even told me he was joining the staff, so how could you expect me to guess his duties? I threw my crystal ball away years ago.'

'Go to sleep.' Simon reached across and turned out Jocelyn's reading light and his voice sounded harsh. 'You're in no mood for a sensible discussion tonight.'

Jocelyn slipped down between the sheets as she felt Simon get up and go across to the other twin bed and lay staring into the dark as she heard him make himself comfortable.

But long after Simon's even breathing told her he was asleep she lay awake. One thing had become abundantly clear during their unsatisfactory conversation. She might be afraid of his implacable will, distrust his motives, but she had unwittingly made a very grave mistake. She had been reckless enough to fall in love with her own husband. Her acceptance of Simon's unexpected proposal of marriage had little or nothing to do with Alan's predicament, she now realized. She might have deceived herself into thinking so once, but the fact had to be faced. She was head over heels in love with Simon and her one determination was to keep this from him at all costs.

It wasn't as difficult to pretend indifference as she imagined, and in the weeks which followed Jocelyn wondered at her own powers as an actress. She and Neville Newton now worked together most of the time, a reorganization which Jocelyn found gave her time to follow her private inclinations, be free to go shopping sometimes where hitherto she had been forced to fit this into a limited lunch-hour. She had time now to consult with Mrs. Telford about domestic matters, arrange menus for dinner parties herself, instead of leaving all the arrangements to the housekeeper, and in the evenings she was not too tired to enjoy the business functions and receptions to which, as heads of the firm, Simon and she received invitations.

Only Janey seemed to be aware of the armour with which Jocelyn had encased herself. She came to dinner one night and while the young doctor whom she had brought along lingered over port and cigars with Simon, she followed Jocelyn to the kitchen and firmly shut the door. The tray for coffee had been left ready by Mrs. Telford and all Jocelyn had to do was switch on the electric percolator and add a jug of cream from the fridge.

Janey wasted no time in coming to the point. 'What's up?' she demanded.

Genuinely surprised, Jocelyn turned, the skirt of her long evening dress swishing softly. 'I don't know what you mean.'

Janey sounded grim. 'I think you do. Have you looked in the mirror lately?'

Deliberately obtuse, Jocelyn turned to face the small mirror on the kitchen wall. 'Not since I changed. I thought this dress was rather nice. What's wrong? Blue usually suits me.'

'It does, and the dress is lovely. I mean you, silly. You don't look your usual sunny self, you're wearing far too much make-up and to put it bluntly you're beginning to look like just another of those empty-headed clothes-horses Wadebridge's churn out by the dozen. And talk like them. All trivia and nothing else.'

'I'm flattered you think I look like one of the agency's successful graduates. I've been made to feel part of the furnishings too often. As to talking nonsense, who wants a woman with brains? If you do have some intelligence it's wiser to hide it.'

Janey studied her friend for several seconds while Jocelyn pretended interest in the progress of the coffee. 'It's not ready yet, so give me a straight answer. All's not as it should be. You don't give me the feeling that "God's in his heaven, all's right with the world," and though I admit at first I thought you were marrying Simon for all the wrong reasons it occurred to me that some of his super assurance might rub off on you, which might make you lose a bit of that king-size inferiority complex. Instead you look positively miserable and you're as brittle as all get out. Not the Jocelyn I know at all.'

'Don't be silly.' Jocelyn tried to instil amusement into her voice. 'I'm sorry if I've talked a lot of drivel this evening. Put it down to closer association with our more

74

empty-headed students now Mrs. Wadebridge has gone. As to my being miserable, that's pure imagination. For the first time in years I can please myself; buy my own clothes, run this flat any way I choose, and I have an easier time all round as far as the office is concerned. Simon has taken on an extra man – Neville Newton. You must meet him. He's clever and he's good-looking. I often leave most of the interviewing to him now, because he's better at judging a girl's possibilities than even Simon's mother used to be.' Jocelyn turned to shake Janey gently by the arm, her face unconsciously pleading. 'Really, I'm just the same as I always was,' she asserted, wishing silently that this was true.

No wonder Janey sensed a difference, Jocelyn thought as the two girls returned to the living-room. All her energies when with Simon were devoted to putting on an act, hiding from his keen eyes her desire to give in to his compelling fascination. He must never discover her overwhelming desire to throw herself into his arms, give up all the pretended indifference and declare her true feelings towards him, for that way led to disaster and could well break the indefinable thread which was all that held them together. It might even cause Simon embarrassment, for since the night when she had accused him of reticence over Neville's admission to the firm Simon had withdrawn behind an insurmountable reserve.

It seemed that Walter Hook shared Janey Rushwick's reservations about Jocelyn's happiness, but unlike Janey he did not try and bring his doubts into the open. His concern took the form of coming in far more frequently than was strictly necessary to consult Jocelyn about matters which she knew to be mere excuses to seek her company, and he formed the habit of hovering in the evenings to insist on walking her home.

Jocelyn was too kind-hearted to try choking off these obviously well-meant attentions, so as Simon at the end of the day was often delayed by last-minute callers she began to accept Walter's company and usually invited him up for a drink when they reached the flat.

This was the busiest time of the year for the agency and if Jocelyn had not had Neville Newton's able assistance she too would have been compelled to do a great deal of overtime, for Wadebridge's were called upon to supply girls to appear not only for advertising fashion shows and holiday stand-ins, but many designers liked to take advantage of the free publicity to be obtained from showing model clothes at functions of national importance. Ascot had just finished and now they were busy arranging for a team of six girls to attend Henley Regatta. Padwyn had proved such a success at Ascot Ladies' Day clad in an unrelieved black dress that at the last minute she had been added to the group going to Henley.

The first of the gravy ads were beginning to appear on hoardings and would be shown on television later in the year. Jocelyn knew from Angie Pendleton that Pablo had been inundated already by other advertising agencies eager to secure Padwyn's services. Simon and Neville between them had gone to Ascot to see that the girls and their escorts circulated and attend to details like transport and expenses. Jocelyn was looking forward to four days by the river away from tension at the office and at home.

It would not be her first visit to the world-famous regatta, for her father's parents had lived near Henley until their deaths two years earlier during a 'flu epidemic. As children she, Janice and Alan had frequently spent summer holidays with their grandparents and Grandpa Ashtead had been a boat builder keenly interested in all forms of water sports. At an early age all three of his grandchildren had been taught the finer points of rowing and Jocelyn was well versed in picking a good crew from a bad.

It wasn't a pastime, however, which appealed to all,

and she prayed the weather would be fine and the models refrain from looking thoroughly bored. Padwyn at least she need not worry about. Surrounded by a bevy of tough, handsome oarsmen she would be in her element even if they were foreign and couldn't speak a word of English. I'd put my money on Padwyn getting across to the High Lama of Shangri-la if he existed, Jocelyn thought, then reprimanded herself for her ill-natured thoughts.

Simon had booked rooms for the entire party at a hotel right in the town centre and to Jocelyn's surprise had insisted on her buying new outfits for herself. She had added a couple of broad-brimmed hats, for informal dress was still frowned upon at the regatta despite the prevailing permissive atmosphere and anyone in jeans and tee-shirts firmly turned away by straw-hatted officials. As she packed, Jocelyn wished Simon had elected to come himself, but maybe he did not yet feel Neville was sufficiently in the picture to look after the agency's affairs for a few days completely on his own.

The first day of the regatta was a disaster as far as showing summer fashions was concerned, for it rained on and off all day and after a brief visit during which the girls were obliged to shelter on the stands or in the refreshment tents, Jocelyn and Neville shepherded them back to the hotel. However, as if to prove that it could be obliging, when Jocelyn awoke on the Friday morning, the weather had turned more kindly and by the time the entire party was ready to walk through the town and over the bridge to the regatta ground the sun was shining and it seemed unbelievable that yesterday the main street had been full of puddles and trees along the river bank, which today danced and twirled in the soft breeze, had hung limp and dripping.

Padwyn, wearing an Edwardian-type gown in deep green and carrying a frilled white and green parasol, was soon the centre of attention and Jocelyn was pleased to see that the cameramen engaged on news coverage took time off from filming the races to spot Wadebridge's latest star as she sauntered through the crowded enclosure. 'With luck,' Jocelyn remarked to Neville over lunch, 'they'll have her in the dailies tomorrow. That dress is by Melisande. They'll be handing out bouquets if we get one of their models in the papers first time out.'

Saturday proved warmer still and even Padwyn, wearing a long dark brown dress in a filmy chiffon, looked wilted by lunchtime. A session in the bar with some rowing enthusiasts from the United States appeared to revive her, and watching from across the crowded marquee, Jocelyn wished she could look as carefree.

To combat the heat she had taken off her hat and was using it as a fan. Neville had provided everyone with iced champagne, but Jocelyn, who considered it an overrated drink, would have given a great deal for a long cool lemonade. She had just discreetly emptied her glass on to the grass under the table for the second time when a voice whispered softly into her ear, 'Wasting good booze again, I see,' and she turned in surprise to meet Simon's twinkling eyes.

Neville was refilling everyone's glass and hadn't yet noticed the latest addition to their party as Simon went on softly, 'Knowing how it gives you a headache, why didn't you ask for something else? Still the shrinking violet when it comes to stating your preferences, aren't you?' then without waiting for a reply he straightened and threaded his way through the crowds towards the bar.

Jocelyn watched his retreating back with mixed feelings, half pain, half pleasure. Pleasure because at the unexpected sight of Simon's face she had felt the now familiar excitement grip her and pain that his first words had been, as usual, ones of censure. He was returning now, a tall glass in his hand, and Jocelyn wondered if she were prejudiced in thinking he seemed to dwarf all the other men round about.

Even Neville Newton, tall, good-looking, assured, could not hold a candle to him, Jocelyn thought as Simon set the glass in front of her, and ice jingled faintly as he said commandingly, 'Drink that, then I'll take you out of this heat. It's like an oven in here and it might be a good idea if all the girls went and sat outside. We don't want to ruin those expensive dresses, and someone has trodden on your skirt. Hadn't you noticed?'

To Jocelyn's dismay as she looked down she saw a large stain on the hemline of her brand-new dress. She had sat sideways on the small folding chair so that the skirt of her long cream dress lay partially on the grass, and someone in the jostling crowds must have stepped on it, for a large and grimy footprint marred the delicate material.

Jocelyn could have wept, for she guessed that no amount of cleaning would remove the grassy stain, and that Simon should have spotted it the instant he appeared added to her mortification. She was dumb with humiliation as he sorted out the party, reassembled them where it was cooler, then leaving Neville in charge guided Jocelyn off along the river bank to where tall trees cast a welcome shade.

There were not quite so many people about, but Jocelyn, still conscious of her flushed face and ruined dress, kept silent as they strolled on, Simon's hand beneath her elbow. At last she looked aside at his unfathomable expression to say, 'I thought you told me you'd be tied up all day.'

'I did, but my appointment for this afternoon was cancelled. It seemed a pity to spend a lovely day like this in London. Sorry to see me? I can't say you were looking as if you were enjoying yourself when I arrived. Why didn't you have lunch outside?'

'Neville arranged it. I don't think he realized how hot it would be in the refreshment tent.'

'Obviously not.' Simon sounded grim. 'And why not tell him more than one glass of champagne gives you a hangover? Honestly, Jocelyn, sometimes I think you need a nursemaid!'

Jocelyn flushed more deeply at his criticism, then a murmur of excitement from the river bank diverted her attention from Simon's reproaches. She put a hand to her eyes, screwing them up as she peered to her right. 'Never mind my many drawbacks. This is the second semi-final for the Grand. One of our college crews and the Americans. The Russians won their heat this morning, so I just mustn't miss this,' and without waiting to find out Simon's reaction Jocelyn pushed forward to get a better view as the competing eights flashed past their viewpoint.

Sixteen oars curving in and out of the sparkling water almost as one turned Jocelyn pink with excitement. Simon, standing filming the race with his ciné camera from behind her, his eyes narrowed as he peered after the rapidly vanishing boats, smiled as Jocelyn asked, 'Did you see? I think we might have won by a canvas. I love rowing, it's like poetry in motion.'

'I know you do,' Simon replied, and took her hand to lead her out of the crowd. 'I haven't forgotten when you were a little girl, you couldn't wait to come in and tell Susan and Mother all about it when you'd been on a visit to your grandparents.'

'Fancy your remembering!' Jocelyn turned to look at him searchingly, but Simon's eyes revealed nothing but a faint amusement at his reminiscences. 'I'm afraid I made a dreadful nuisance of myself, always popping in and out to see Susan when we were little, but she had far more patience with me than Janice ever had and I used to come and tell her all my news.'

'Don't start apologizing. Susan enjoyed your company, otherwise I daresay she'd soon have choked you off. Come to that, we all liked to see you. You weren't half so self-conscious in those days even when I was around.'

Jocelyn gave him a nervous glance, but Simon's face

was unreadable. Meeting her anxious eyes he smiled faintly and said lightly, 'Stop looking so apprehensive, Kitten, and relax. Take a leaf out of Padwyn's book for once. Look at her — she doesn't give a damn for anyone.'

They had almost reached the rest of the party again and Jocelyn could see Padwyn, her arms hooked into two blazer-clad arms as she posed with several of the oarsmen to have a photograph taken, and Jocelyn recognized Steve Wells, Pablo Pendleton's chief assistant behind the camera. She turned to Simon and as if he had read her thoughts he said, 'Yes, Steve's standing in today. Pablo and Angie have taken the baby to Wales for the week-end. Pablo's father is a semi-invalid, doesn't travel much these days, and of course the family are anxious to see the new grandchild.'

The day's rowing finally drew to a close and everyone went back to the hotel to take off their borrowed plumes. Simon had booked a table for dinner and dancing at one of the larger riverside hotels, and Jocelyn sighed as she hung up the ruined dress, wishing they could dine quietly alone while this more amenable mood of Simon's lasted. She had showered and made up her face before Simon came upstairs to change and was sitting clad in a light dressing-gown brushing her hair when he finally arrived.

'Padwyn's apparently invited about a dozen crew members to join us. The Americans are rowing in the final against the Russians tomorrow, so it's early to bed for them, poor lads. I reckon there'll be twenty or so of us, but as there are three vehicles with mine, Neville's and the mini-bus, we should manage to squeeze in.'

He was taking off his jacket as he spoke, loosening his tie and unbuttoning his shirt. The forthcoming dinner party, however, had been briefly forgotten by Jocelyn. 'So Lady Margaret lost. I really thought we had them. What a shame! This will make the third year running the

Grand Challenge Trophy has gone out of the country. And to think the British introduced the sport to most of the rest of the world!'

Simon laughed and coming up behind took her by the shoulders. 'Disappointed, are you? Never mind, maybe we'll have better luck next year. Remember we're a small country compared with Russia and America. They've several more millions to choose from, so it's not to be wondered at that they're world-beaters in sport.'

He withdrew his hands, but not before Jocelyn felt the old familiar response, the almost irresistible urge to turn and catch his hands in her own, lay her cheek against the back of them. Already the impulse was waning as he asked, 'Finished with the bathroom?' and at her nod disappeared to wash before changing into a dinner suit.

Everyone was ready when they got downstairs to the lobby with the exception of Padwyn. She kept them all waiting a further ten minutes, but the effect of her entrance down the wide staircase wearing a starkly simple black evening dress had every male eye in the foyer on her, Jocelyn noted, including Simon's. She shivered despite the fact she was wearing a light shawl over her bare shoulders and the evening air was mild.

Rather to her surprise, however, when the entire party had been sorted out, Jocelyn found herself sitting beside Simon in his roomy car with three of the girls occupying the rear seat, though quite how he had manoeuvred this arrangement and why, Jocelyn could not guess. True, he was usually meticulous in his attentions when they were in public. Whatever his real reason for marrying her, he had apparently no intention of letting anyone guess theirs was anything but a conventional marriage, entered into for the usual reasons.

Everyone was in holiday mood and the large dinner party went off better than Jocelyn had anticipated, owing partly to plenty of good food and wine, Simon's dexterity in welding together a body of people with very little in common and, Jocelyn admitted to herself, in part to Padwyn's disarming manner with the men. Elocution lessons had obliterated a good deal of her accent and rapid success in a competitive field had removed the last of Padwyn's provincial gaucheness.

Her lively mind, quick wit and fund of amusing stories kept everyone round the table in fits of laughter. She was also a born mimic and her impression of one of the leading photographers in the business, now well past his prime, made even Simon's lips twitch, though he remarked quietly, 'He's still got plenty of influence, so don't deal with him too unkindly, Padwyn, for your own sake,' before he rose and pulled Jocelyn to her feet.

They had circled the floor twice before Jocelyn's pulse beat returned to normal. She was concentrating so hard on following Simon's lead with legs that felt as if they had turned to indiarubber that she was quite startled when he suddenly drew her close, laid his cheek against the top of her head and as the band continued to play a dreamy waltz whispered softly, 'You're not facing a firing squad, so just relax.'

Jocelyn let out a gasp and went limp in his arms so that Simon tightened his hold, saying laughingly, 'You're either one thing or the other, aren't you, Kitten? I said relax, not collapse! We'd cause quite a scene if I had to carry you bodily off the floor.'

Jocelyn smiled and looked saucily into her husband's eyes. 'I thought you liked instant obedience. I was only trying to be a dutiful wife. Sorry if I overdid it.'

'Now you sound as affected as all the others, so drop the smart talk or I'll really live up to your assumption that I go for total obedience. And another thing,' Simon stopped speaking as he leant close, 'isn't that Padwyn's perfume you're wearing? I really think your own suits you better.'

Jocelyn looked away, feeling the old familiar hopelessness at the implacable note in Simon's voice. She gazed across at Padwyn, envying her carefree self-as-surance, for one word of criticism was sufficient to drive away her own precarious poise. If only just once Simon would give a word of praise, boost her self-confidence by a compliment. Instead he seemed to take pleasure in stifling every effort she made to please him. She had gone to a good deal of trouble to find out what brand of perfume Padwyn favoured and buying a small bottle in the hope that it would be a rewarding change, even give her flagging confidence a lift. The heavier, more soph-isticated perfume had seemed a pleasant contrast to the light, flowery scent she usually wore.

Apparently Simon did not agree and they finished the dance in silence. Jocelyn was not sorry when the music stopped and they could walk back to the table, for all her pleasure in Simon's unexpected company had vanished and it was with a heavy heart that she managed to smile and joke her way through the remainder of the evening. They all had to be up early the next morning to attend a special service in the parish church, so much to Jocelyn's relief the party broke up relatively early.

When they reached the hotel, on the pretext of having a headache, she went straight up to bed leaving Simon having a nightcap with Neville. When he finally came to bed Jocelyn lay with closed eyes pretending to be already asleep. What an ending to a day which had promised so well! Simon had earlier seemed so genuinely pleased to be able to join the party, had even singled her out for special attentiveness, and once again she seemed to have spoiled things. Yet she couldn't have foreseen his unwarranted annoyance about the perfume. For some reason it had made him withdraw again behind his barrier of polite reserve. Why did she always have to put her foot in it?

She was roused by the arrival of morning tea and the sound of Simon whistling as he shaved, and she was half-way through her second cup when he emerged from the bathroom. His morning greeting was cheery, but Jocelyn sensed that indefinable iciness in his manner. Gone was the companion of yesterday afternoon who had laughed at her enthusiasm over the outcome of the semi-finals, teased and held her close during that first dance.

Jocelyn had bathed and was brushing her teeth when he tapped on the bathroom door. 'See you downstairs in half an hour,' he called out. 'I'm going for a stroll round the block before breakfast.'

Quickly Jocelyn dressed in a simple brown skirt and frilly cream blouse, combed and lacquered her hair, applied make-up and packed their suitcases in record time. It would not be wise to ignore Simon's command, she decided as she picked up her handbag, and then her eye fell on the disputed bottle of perfume. It landed in the waste bin with a faint plop as she picked up the room key and went to join the others.

The large table in the dining-room was already occupied as Simon and Jocelyn walked in, the models enviously watching the others eating eggs and bacon as they toyed with their own meagre breakfasts of black coffee and melba toast. On the pretext that she must see the dressers, Jocelyn quickly swallowed fruit juice and cereal before escaping to supervise the packing of the gowns worn on the previous three days along with all the accessories.

'No need for you to hang about,' she told the two middle-aged sisters who invariably undertook the roles of dressers and packers for the agency. 'I'll see to the packing of today's outfits myself and Mr. Wadebridge and I can bring them back this evening. The van's already here, so I suggest you find a couple of the porters and get this lot loaded. I'll see you both tomorrow morning, then we can go through the whole lot and see if there's been any damage done before they're returned.'

Jocelyn's more than usually subdued demeanour appeared to pass unnoticed as they trooped down to join the other worshippers for the morning service. The church was packed and Jocelyn forgot her bruised feelings as strong young voices joined in the hymns and responses. She glanced around at rows of blazer-clad men, many wearing the ties of famous rowing institutions interspersed with the summery dresses of their wives, sisters, mothers and sweethearts. The lessons were read by two elderly ex-oarsmen whom Jocelyn vaguely recognized as having seen several times during the last three days, though she was unfamiliar with their names.

By the time the last races were over, the girls taken back to the hotel, their finery packed away and they and their escorts packed into the mini-bus, Jocelyn felt physically exhausted. Neville and Padwyn had left together in Neville's car and once the mini-bus had departed only Simon and Jocelyn remained to load the last dress boxes into the back of the car and their suitcases into the boot.

As he was paying the bill Simon asked suddenly, 'Shall we eat before we leave?'

Jocelyn had no wish to linger and answered more curtly than she realized, 'Must we? I don't know about you, but I'm not very hungry. I can whip up an omelette or something when we get home.'

'As you like.' Simon's voice was expressionless as he slipped his cheque book back into his pocket and led the way out to the car. Why did I say 'home'? Jocelyn thought dismally as she adjusted her seat belt. Just habit, I guess, because it's merely the place where Simon and I happen to live. Home is where the heart is, and Simon's not interested in hearts.

CHAPTER FOUR

THOUGH she dressed and made up with her usual care next morning, signs of her inward turmoil were apparently visible to one pair of discerning eyes, for Walter's first words were, 'What's the matter, Jocelyn? If it's anything I can put right you know you've only to say the word.'

Jocelyn looked up into his anxious eyes and smiled faintly. 'Just a headache, Walter. Not to worry.'

He remained gazing down, however, as if unconvinced, so that Jocelyn got to her feet and in an effort to reassure him, dispel the worried look from his spaniel brown eyes, laid a hand affectionately on his shoulder just as the door swung unexpectedly open and Simon came in.

He stopped, a heavy frown making his black brows into one thick line of disapproval as he said with calculated civility, 'When you two can spare a minute I'd like to have a list of what damage, if any, has been done to the collections we took to Henley, then Walter can let me have a breakdown of the expenses, etc., for each firm,' and he was gone before they could reply.

After a moment's embarrassed silence Walter moved towards the door, but once there he stopped to speak. 'Like that, is it?' and to Jocelyn's surprise he looked more amused than contrite. 'I suspect Simon's got a worse headache than you, dear girl.'

What could Walter mean? Jocelyn wondered as she hurried to carry out Simon's instructions. There was no time now, though, to think out Walter's extraordinary reaction. What amazed her had been Simon's, for he had undoubtedly seen her hand lying on Walter's shoulder and his irrational rudeness could only have been due to this. Surely though, he couldn't possibly be jealous of dear, uncomplicated Walter? It was such a crazy idea,

Jocelyn dismissed it from her mind.

They had just finished their evening meal and Jocelyn was in the kitchen waiting for the coffee to percolate when the telephone rang and a few minutes later Simon's head appeared round the kitchen door. 'Angie on the telephone. She's just got junior tucked up and wants a quick word.'

Jocelyn, with a, 'Keep your eye on the coffee,' went quickly through the door Simon was holding wide to speak to her friend.

As soon as she picked up the receiver Angie Pendleton's voice sounded in her ear. 'That you, Jo? We got back from Wales in time for the baby's early evening feed, so I thought I'd phone before I start getting our own supper. We've fixed up details about the christening. Can you and Simon come for a meal tomorrow so I can tell you all the plans? We've decided to have it in Wales on account of my father-in-law, but I'll tell you all that when I see you. Think you could be here by eight?'

'Of course, but won't we be a frightful nuisance? You've enough to do coping with a new baby without supper guests.'

'Nonsense,' Angie's laughing voice came back over the line. 'In any case, I know you and Simon won't object if the meal isn't in the Cordon Bleu class. I'll do my usual — throw something into a casserole and just hope for the best.'

'Well, if you're certain, I'd love to come. Simon too,' Jocelyn added hastily, 'but if he can't make it I'll give you a ring tomorrow.'

Jocelyn hung up just as Simon appeared with the coffee tray. 'What was that about "if Simon can make it"?'

'Angie! She wants us to go over for supper tomorrow. Apparently Philip Robin Julius's christening is to be held in Wales. I've accepted and told Angie I'd let her know if you couldn't manage it.'

'Of course I shall come, but is that really what they're going to call the poor little perisher?' Simon's voice held real amusement. 'What on earth possessed them to pick a combination like that?'

'Philip because both Angie and Pablo like it; Robin after Angie's father, Julius after Pablo's,' Jocelyn explained succinctly.

'Well, I only hope he forgives them when he's old enough to understand.' Simon still sounded amused at the Pendletons' choice of names for their son. He poured out a cup of coffee, added milk and handed it to Jocelyn, saying with a twinkle in his eye, 'Make sure you enunciate clearly when you tell his reverence the grim tidings at the ceremony, or he may get christened almost anything, since the minister will in all probability be Welsh-speaking. And pray he's in no way hard of hearing.'

Jocelyn saw the funny side and found herself laughing quite naturally with Simon, for the first time in days not on her guard. 'You're right, of course. It seems rather a long handle for such a small baby. Perhaps he'll grow up to fit it. It's funny, but people always seem to me to grow into their names.'

Simon reached across and ruffled her hair. 'What nonsense you talk sometimes! Drink your coffee and let's watch Panorama. They've chosen quite an interesting topic as their main subject tonight.'

He switched on the television and came to sit beside her on the settee. Jocelyn snuggled down, wishing life was always so uncomplicated as it was right this moment. She sneaked a look at Simon's absorbed expression and wished she had not become so emotionally involved with the man at her side. When he felt in the mood he treated her with an off-hand affection which if anything increased her shyness. Despite several weeks of intimacy with this man who with apparently supreme indifference to her innermost feelings had persuaded her into marriage Jocelyn felt no nearer to him. Simon was invulnerable, she thought with a small sigh as she slipped her cup and saucer quietly back on to the coffee table, trying not to distract his attention from the programme. Simon must have registered the small movement, however, for he turned and asked softly, 'Anything you want, Kitten? Shall I reheat the coffee?'

Jocelyn shook her head, unwilling to trust her voice. Why couldn't this apparent consideration have real depth? But no one could speak as Simon had spoken this morning when he had found her and Walter together if he felt anything more than a possessive sort of jealousy. And she had only herself to blame for her present unhappiness. Simon had never spoken one word about love, nor asked her to love in return. She must continue to conceal from him her true reactions to living in the shadow of his irresistible personality.

It made a pleasant change the following evening to enter the homely relaxed atmosphere of the Pendletons' mews flat. Angie Pendleton might have joked about 'throwing a few things into a casserole', but she was in fact an excellent cook and despite her preoccupation with the new baby had found time to set the table attractively with cream linen mats, gleaming cutlery and glassware set off by a shallow bowl of creamy rosebuds. A succulent ragout accompanied by green salad was preceded by avocado pear with a vinaigrette dressing. Angie apologized for the lack of a dessert, but since she provided a cheese board which made Simon's eyes gleam with appreciation, her apologies were brushed aside as Pablo looked laughingly across the table and said, 'My good girl, you know as well as I do that sweets don't interest me, and I'm sure Jocelyn and Simon don't care a tinker's cuss either. Sit still while I make coffee.'

Angie laughingly obeyed and the companionable foursome sat around the small oval dining-table long after the cheeses had been sampled and the coffee pot emptied. Plans for the baby's christening in the village church near

Pablo's old home were discussed, and Simon and Jocelyn promised that nothing should stop them travelling to Wales for the occasion.

'Mother will be delighted to put you up,' Pablo added. 'We've plenty of room and she loves having visitors now she and Father get around so little. It's to be a very quiet affair, just Angie's uncle and my brother as the other god-parents and one or two old family friends to wet the baby's head afterwards.'

'What about your sister?' Jocelyn asked Angie. 'Won't she be able to fly over? I'm sure you'd rather she were Philip's godmother.'

Angie Pendleton laughed and patted Jocelyn on the hand as she pushed back her chair. 'Jo, really! You must be joking. You know Netta as well as I do. Would you expect her to fly all the way from Canada just for a vil-lage christening party? If we could have made arrange-ments to hold it in the crypt at the House of Commons or somewhere equally impressive she'd be here like a shot, but for a quiet, family affair with no national publicity, oh, dear me, no! So put your scruples away.'

Any reservation Jocelyn might have felt vanished and she half smiled to herself as she helped Angie clear the table. Too true she knew Angie's sister well, for Robinetta Snow had once been one of Wadebridge's top models and had come very close to ruining Angie's chances of hap-piness by her selfishness. At one time she had professed that she wanted to marry Pablo herself and Angie had been prepared to sacrifice herself for her younger sister's sake. Chance in the form of a handsome, wealthy and influential Canadian had saved the day, for after a whirl-wind courtship Robinetta had married him, leaving Angie free to follow her heart and admit at last to Pablo that her pretended indifference was a lie.

As they washed up together Angie confided to Jocelyn that she and Pablo were in something of a quandary. 'This flat is far too small with a baby's things around and

I can't make up my mind what to do. We've the chance of buying the place next door, which would give us twice the space, but they're asking the earth for the lease and it's been empty for over a year. You should see the inside! It looks as if it's not been cleaned in years and it's had nothing done by way of modernization. No central heating and the oddest bathroom you ever saw – right out of Dickens. We've also had the offer of a super flat about half an hour's walk away, but there would be no garden there either, and I would so love a wee patch. Advise me, Jo. Of course, my ideal would be a house in the country, but then I'd see hardly anything of Pablo.'

Jocelyn dried a glass carefully. 'I think the place next door would be my choice. If it's so badly in need of reconstruction you can have a field day. You could knock the two places into one and really go to town with your own ideas. A flat even half an hour away might make you feel very lonely and cut off. Here, right on the spot, Pablo can pop up to see you any time he wants.'

Angie nodded as she washed and rinsed the last plate and put it on the drainer. 'You're right, of course, but come and look at next door. I've got the key and we've half an hour or so before Philip will want his feed.'

In the end Simon and Pablo accompanied the two girls into the dilapidated building next door. Angie had not exaggerated; a lot needed doing apart from the obvious modifications of an entrance through into their flat and the complete renovation of the bathroom which held a gas geyser of mind-bending antiquity. Everywhere paint and paper were peeling, and large holes where the aged plaster had broken away gaped in several of the rooms. The original casements had never been replaced and in comparison with the light living quarters next door this flat seemed unusually gloomy. To make this long-neglected dwelling comfortable and labour-saving would be a mammoth task, Jocelyn could see.

Simon inspected the whole place thoroughly and

when they reassembled in what had obviously been the kitchen he stood, arms on hips, looking around at the grimy stone sink and greasy gas cooker before airing his views. 'Make them an offer, Pablo, but nothing like what they're asking. And get a good architect's opinion first. Let him give you a rough estimate of what it will cost to make it habitable and draw up some plans. If you do buy, with a reputable name behind you planning permission will be given that much quicker. In any case, building regulations are changing all the time. You want to find out precisely what you can or can't do before you commit yourself.'

'It's a challenge for Angie, you must admit,' Jocelyn remarked as they were driving home. 'With double the space they can have a beautiful home.'

Her voice must have been unconsciously wistful, for Simon turned to look at her and reached out to squeeze her fingers. 'You sound green with envy, Kitten. Has it been a bit of a come-down to take over a modern flat without even a say in its decoration?'

Jocelyn hastily refuted the assertion. 'Of course not. What time would I have to choose wallpapers, run up curtains? In any case, I'm not sure it's quite my scene.' Trust Simon, she thought, to come so near the truth.

Though they were busy as usual at the agency during the next few days, Jocelyn became aware of changes in the behaviour of two of her closest colleagues. Walter Hook suddenly stopped acting like an over-anxious St. Bernard and Neville Newton's usual smiling good humour and assurance seem temporarily to have deserted him.

The answer to Neville's curious change in manner came one evening a couple of days later when Jocelyn and Simon were on their way to a reception being given to launch a new American cosmetic. As they threaded their way through heavy traffic Jocelyn asked, 'Have we really room here for yet another brand name? I should have thought the British market was flooded already, and customers are often strangely unwilling to change from a product they know and have used for years.'

'With Padwyn on the advertisements and commercials they stand a very good chance,' Simon replied carelessly, 'though of course Neville's a bit sick about her being chosen by the firm. If she's a winner here they'll soon spirit her over to the States, and he's well aware that she may take a long-term contract with them and vanish from the London scene. I knew he'd burn his fingers when he offered her a room at his flat.'

Jocelyn was silent as she digested this information. It gave an answer to much which had perplexed her, and not only Neville's unusual abstraction. Walter, Simon and two men with marked transatlantic accents had been in consultation on several occasions of late, but fearing a rebuff, Jocelyn had asked no questions. The daily conferences Simon had held with his mother had been discontinued when Jocelyn took over her work and she was often forced to pick up information on the agency's latest plans more by chance than anything else.

Why was Simon suddenly being so forthcoming? Jocelyn wondered as she turned to study his profile. 'Will she take a contract if it's offered?'

'She'd be a fool if she didn't,' Simon replied shortly, 'and our Padwyn's no fool. It's a fantastic opportunity for a newcomer. Yes, I know she's done extremely well with the gravy ads,' he went on as Jocelyn opened her mouth to interrupt, 'but compared with this the pay was peanuts. The firm mean to win or bust, and personally I think they'll make it. Their products really are good *and* they're expensive.' He stopped to throw Jocelyn a sardonic smile. 'Haven't you noticed, Kitten, that's often a good selling angle? Women are in the main suspicious of anything that's offered to them at a reasonable price. Their immediate reaction is that if it's cheap then it can't be any good.'

'What idiots you make us sound!' Jocelyn laughed, but there was little amusement in her voice. 'Not got a very high opinion of the female sex, have you, Simon?'

'Don't get your hackles up, Kitten.' There was just a hint of mockery in Simon's deep tones. 'I meant nothing personal when I said women prefer their luxuries to be expensive. You shouldn't be so touchy. Sweet unreasonableness is part of your charm, you know.'

This last comment kept Jocelyn effectively silent, and when they reached their destination they were soon swept apart as Simon, throwing her a quick, 'sorry, sweet, back in a minute', was buttonholed by a tall man who took him by the arm and bore him away in the direction of the bar. Jocelyn found herself standing alone at one side of the brilliantly lit room, watching the other guests circulate. Suddenly she became aware of an enormous blown-up photograph covering most of one wall. It dominated the room, and as Jocelyn almost absentmindedly accepted a glass of wine from a hovering waiter she found her attention captured and held by the unusual attitude in which Padwyn's charms had been photographed, well used though she was to the various devices which were employed to catch the public's eye.

'Quite extraordinarily impressive, isn't it?' a voice said quietly into her left ear, and Jocelyn swung round to find that Neville Newton had joined her and that his eyes unashamedly sad, were fixed on the huge photograph opposite. He had both hands deep in his trouser pockets and he might never have laid eyes on Padwyn in the flesh as he went on with his assessment of her photograph. 'She's a natural, of course. Some girls have it, some haven't. It's just an accident of birth. The girl's lucky, because she's no beauty when you study her feature by feature, yet she holds and attracts one's attention.'

He suddenly seemed to pull himself together, for he turned to look directly at Jocelyn and his eyes held a curious mixture of sorrow and exhilaration. 'I suppose I was an optimist, expecting her to give up such a chance. Has Simon told you?'

Jocelyn nodded. 'Padwyn's signed, then?'

'About an hour ago; on the proverbial dotted line. She'll be leaving very soon.'

Jocelyn placed her glass on a convenient ledge, linked her arm in Neville's and deliberately changed the subject. 'I'm famished, Neville – I only got coffee and a sausage roll at lunch-time. I see there's a buffet. Let's go and have something to eat.'

For a moment Neville stiffened, then Jocelyn felt the resistance ebb as with a bitter note in his usually pleasant poice, he agreed, 'Yes, why not? Eat, drink and be merry, for soon my bonny will lie over the ocean.'

Some minutes later, with loaded plates, they found a quiet corner in which to enjoy the best the buffet could offer. Jocelyn had overridden Neville's assertion that he wasn't hungry. Under her instructions the waiter had served them enormous hot chicken and mushroom patties fairly oozing with sauce, sliced tomatoes seasoned with herbs and chives, lettuce tossed in a French dressing and asparagus, green and tender dripping with butter.

Neville laughed as they picked up their knives and forks, a note of genuine amusement in his voice. 'If you can get through all that I'll take my hat off to you. Where do you put it, Jo? You're as thin as a lath.'

Jocelyn's eyes twinkled as, her mouth full, she saw with satisfaction that Neville's natural sense of humour had taken over and he looked near normal again. Ten minutes later, she laid her knife and fork down with a sigh. 'That was marvellous.' She glanced briefly to see Neville's plate as clean as her own. 'You were hungry after all.'

Neville offered a cigarette and as she shook her head, lit one for himself. 'Yes, I guess I was.' His expression softened. 'It just needed a well-meaning soul to remind me.'

Jocelyn wrinkled her nose in an expression of disgust. 'I

guess I deserved the reminder that I'm inclined to think food is the panacea for all troubles, but honestly, things never look so gloomy on a full stomach.'

'Agreed.' Neville got to his feet as he spoke. 'To prove you right let's go and join the rest of this circus. Have you met the kingpin who laid all this on?'

'No, not yet.' Jocelyn got to her feet, shook out her skirt and picked up her small evening bag. 'What's he like?'

'Quite a decent fellow, as a matter of fact – but you shall judge for yourself.'

It took them some time to make their way through the crowded room to where, under the huge photograph, the American representative in charge of the evening's festivities was standing, Padwyn at his side looking strangely unexcited by her good fortune. Simon, on the American's other side, stopped speaking as he spotted Neville and Jocelyn arm in arm and stepped forward to ask in a stage whisper, 'Where've you been? I've been looking for you. This is business, not pleasure, I might remind you.' In normal tones he turned to say smoothly, 'You know my associate, Neville Newton, Mr. Philbrick, but I don't think you've met my wife.'

Jocelyn found her hand shaken firmly and her eyes looking into the kindly ones of her host. He was little taller than herself with that well scrubbed look common to most Americans, and while he was making her welcome Jocelyn found herself subjected to a shrewd appraisal.

He drew Jocelyn to one side where a display of the company's products were on show. 'Now, I hear you're a young lady who knows her job, but that's obvious by the way Miss Padwyn's got along so well under your care. What about marketing? Know anything about that? I'd like your opinion both as a woman and as a knowledgeable critic. Tell me, what do you think of these ideas for packaging? I don't suppose you've tried our cosmetics yet.'

Reluctantly Jocelyn had to admit that until 'his moment she had not even laid eyes on the new brand lines. They spent some time examining and discussing the lotions, creams, conditioners and cosmetics of various kinds before Simon strolled over to join them.

'This little lady's no fool and has given me some great ideas,' Mr. Philbrick commented, and Simon slanted Jocelyn a faintly ironic smile. 'We never thought in terms of miniature packs except as samples. Mrs. Wadebridge has come up with a notion for a small handbag size in slim zippered containers fitted up like a manicure case to hold only what a woman needs for a re-make when she's away from home. Say a small phial of perfume, powder, lipstick, eye-shadow, foundation, cleansing lotion and tissues. Then all our various preparations to be available in boxes of say half a dozen miniature sizes for replacement. What I can't understand is why our ideas department back home didn't come up with such a scheme. Goodness knows we pay them enough. Yet it takes Mrs. Wadebridge only a minute to spot a new possibility.'

Mr. Philbrick turned to beam approval on the scarlet-cheeked Jocelyn. 'I suppose you wouldn't care to cut adrift from this husband of yours and join our company?' he suggested.

'Not a chance,' Simon said before a tongue-tied Jocelyn could think up an answer to this unexpected proposition. 'She's much too valuable, in more senses than one,' and he deliberately put an arm round Jocelyn's shoulders.

Mr. Philbrick laughed heartily and winked good-humouredly. 'Sure! I get it. And I couldn't agree more. A happy marriage comes before business and you can't enjoy that three thousand miles apart. But if you won't join us,' he said directly to Jocelyn, 'I insist you accept the gift of a selection of our products. At least then we'll have one, I hope, satisfied customer to start us off on the right foot in the U.K.'

Jocelyn stammered an almost incoherent expression of

thanks, acutely aware of Simon's arm still draped around her shoulders. As they moved to rejoin Neville and Padwyn deep in a quiet conversation together, Simon lowered his arm to link a hand through the crook of Jocelyn's bare elbow. He was obviously determined she was not going to slip away and disappear a second time.

When they left over an hour later, an imposing leather vanity case fitted with every type of cosmetic for beautifying and preserving a lady's complexion reposed on the rear seat. 'You seem to have made a hit with our astute Mr. Philbrick,' Simon remarked. 'Full marks for making such a clever suggestion about the miniature beauty kits.'

'Not very clever really,' Jocelyn replied. 'Every normal working girl has to carry around what she needs to re-do her face during the hours she spends at her place of work, so why not put them on the market in a convenient package? If the colour blends are interchangeable there are no limits to the permutations of creams and powders, lipstick and eye-shadow, for instance. All you'd have to do is buy one of the holders and a box of the small tubes or whatever in your own particular shade. I can't think why someone hasn't thought of it long ago.'

'The fact remains that nobody has – until tonight, that is. You've hidden talents even I never dreamed you possessed,' Simon congratulated her, but Jocelyn inwardly writhed at the faint amusement in his deep voice. This wasn't what she wanted from Simon, this half indulgent, half admiring way of complimenting her as though she were a small child who had excelled in her performance at an end-of-term concert.

She was amazed to hear her own voice say quite acidly, 'Stop humouring me as if I were a little girl. It's quite unnecessary.'

Surprised at her bravery in speaking out, she was aware that Simon shot her a sharp glance before his eyes returned to the road ahead. The rest of the journey was completed in silence and when they let themselves into the flat Jocelyn experienced a moment of wry amusement as Simon, a conciliatory note in his voice, said, 'Go to bed. You're obviously overtired. I'll bring you a hot drink in a few minutes.'

The next two weeks went by smoothly enough with only the usual day-to-day irritations cropping up to keep the staff of Wadebridge's on their toes. Collections were being got ready all over London and Jocelyn had more bookings for girls to model the new season's designs than ever before, so Neville's help in sharing the work load was invaluable. Since the night of the launching of the new American cosmetic he had not once directly referred to Padwyn's imminent departure for America, and Jocelyn was reluctant to force his confidence. If he was suffering from disappointment he hid it well, and obviously any probing into his personal affairs would be impertinent, to say the least.

Jocelyn could hardly tell Neville she too was a victim of unrequited love, for Simon in public gave no indication of being anything other than a devoted if not over-demonstrative husband. In any case, what red-blooded girl would care to admit that she had been married more for her usefulness than her charms? So Jocelyn tried to ease the inner dejection she guessed Neville must be concealing by being extra friendly, by keeping him busy and as far away from Padwyn's vicinity during business hours as possible.

She had of course no control over Neville's movements once away from the agency, but the sight of Padwyn preparing to pack for an unlimited stay abroad right under his very eye must rub salt into the wound. On several occasions, therefore, Jocelyn persuaded Neville to return to have a meal at the flat and knowing Janey to be at a loose end with her doctor away on a course, Jocelyn invited her too, until at last Simon, an ironic smile in his eyes, asked, 'Not trying your hand at matchmaking, I hope? You'd be wasting your time.'

Jocelyn flushed as she recognized the all too familiar note of amused disparagement in Simon's voice. Why couldn't he give her credit for being merely sympathetic to the perplexities of their friends' problems without making a couple of invitations to dinner seem like interference in other people's private affairs? Their own uncomfortable relationship should have made Simon more sympathetic instead of critical, but apparently it didn't.

No matter how hard she tried it seemed to Jocelyn she could never earn Simon's wholehearted approval and support except within the confines of the agency where now he appeared to have conceded confidence in her abilities. If he felt something vital was missing from his marriage, however, he gave no sign, baffling Jocelyn daily by his matter-of-fact attitude. They might have been married for years, she thought resentfully one morning when having brought in early tea, he kissed her absentmindedly as he handed her the cup and saucer to announce casually, 'I think I shall take Padwyn over to the States when she goes next week. I can see her settled, look up a few of our contacts in New York and then have a couple of days with Mother. I know you and Neville will be able to manage without me. As far as I can see nothing of any special importance is liable to crop up, so it will just be a case of seeing that the wheels keep turning smoothly.'

No question of taking her along too, Jocelyn thought resentfully as she sipped the hot tea and watched, a mutinous look in her eyes as Simon opened the wardrobe door and proceeded to select a tie from the rack. What Neville thought of Simon's arrangement, Jocelyn was at a loss to know. He displayed nothing except polite interest when told how and with whom Padwyn was travelling merely asking one or two pertinent questions about the running of the agency during Simon's absence and remarking casually to Jocelyn as he was on the point of leaving her office, 'We shall have to find a new flatmate. It's on the cards Padwyn may stay in the States, and even if she does return I imagine she'll want a pad of her own. No pun intended,' he finished with a grin as he closed the door behind him.

Jocelyn looked thoughtfully at the closed door for several minutes after his departure. If he was nursing a bruised heart as she suspected, Neville was concealing it well. She hoped her own histrionic abilities were as adequate.

It was as well the agency was so busy, Jocelyn thought as she got on with her many tasks. During the day at least she had little time to dwell on the frustrations of an unsatisfactory personal life. Neville volunteered to take the travellers to London Airport on the day of departure, and suspecting he wanted to be with Padwyn to the last possible moment, Jocelyn raised no objections at being left out of the arrangements to see Simon and Padwyn off.

She was surprised as they breakfasted together on the morning of his departure to hear Simon say, 'Be good while I'm away, Kitten. Don't let that soft heart of yours lead you into dispensing too much tea and sympathy.'

Jocelyn looked up, a morsel of toast halfway to her mouth in unashamed surprise. At her wide-eyed stare of astonishment Simon grinned, a lopsided smile quirking one corner of his mouth higher than the other as he asked, 'Think I don't notice the soothing noises you make to anyone you consider a lame duck? You waste your pity half the time, so don't get carried away during my absence. Most of your protégées are far better equipped to take care of themselves than you are yourself, so I should be annoyed to come home and find you'd allowed your good nature to be exploited.'

Jocelyn, baffled by this astonishing and unexpected diatribe, remained silent. Simon drained his cup and got to his feet. 'All right. Kitten, forget it. Just be a good girl while I'm away and I'll bring you back the Statue of

Liberty as a souvenir.'

There he went again! Jocelyn thought indignantly as she cleared the breakfast table; treating her like a half-witted child. Not that she had responded to Simon's injuction with anything even remotely resembling intelligence, but she had been too surprised to show her usual quick comprehension. No wonder Simon had dismissed the matter since he appeared to be getting no commonsense reaction.

Apparently, however, he hadn't quite forgotten the one-sided conversation at breakfast. When he came into her office later that morning to tell her they were ready to leave he bewildered her yet again by taking her into his arms, kissing her firmly on the mouth and reiterating his warning. 'Don't forget what I told you earlier,' he commanded before he kissed her again, making her pulses race, then as he reached the door he turned and smiled across the room, a gesture which made Jocelyn put a hand on the desk to steady herself. 'You have my permission to miss me while I'm away,' he grinned, and his hard eyes softened as they lingered on her slight figure. 'See you!' and he was gone, leaving Jocelyn with a wild desire to run after him, throw her arms around his neck and beg him to take her along too, or better still, let Padwyn find her own way across the Atlantic.

But the thought of Simon's reaction to such undisciplined conduct was even more restraining than the sensation it would have caused in reception. The amusement of the staff at such odd behaviour would be as nothing compared with the icy set-down by Simon at any ill-advised display of emotion. Jocelyn shuddered at the mere thought of the look of surprised disgust which she envisaged would be her reward for an exhibition of typical feminine vapours. Simon might indulge it in a valuable client, never in a wife.

Jocelyn had to be content with watching from her window as Simon handed Padwyn carefully into Neville's car in the street below, and sighed as it disappeared in a tangle of traffic three minutes later. The following morning with no Simon to bring tea and wake her as usual, she slept late and was only in the office on time by showering and dressing at breakneck speed and scrapping breakfast altogether.

She was halfway through the morning's work when she discovered that her engagement ring was missing, but a call to Mrs. Telford revealed that in her haste she had left it on the wash-basin in the bathroom. 'I found it a few minutes ago,' the housekeeper reassured her. 'I'll put it on the pin tray in your bedroom.'

Jocelyn thanked her and rang off with a sigh of relief. Up to now she had been particularly careful of the beautiful ring Simon had given her, knowing how prone she was to forget where she had put down such small items of jewellery as she possessed. She would never forgive herself were she to lose it, despite Simon's earlier assurance that he would willingly buy her another should such a contingency arise.

When Neville returned from the airport he seemed much as usual, though during the afternoon Jocelyn thought his manner slightly subdued. Had Simon not read her a lecture that very morning about being over-sympathetic, Jocelyn might have invited him back for a drink. Instead she left the office earlier than usual while Neville was still coping with some last-minute commissions Simon had left behind.

She arrived home to find Mrs. Telford just laying the supper table for one. 'Don't bother,' Jocelyn said quickly. 'Since I'll be alone, I think I'll have supper on a tray in front of the television, if you don't mind – and,' she added as Mrs. Telford smiled and turned to go back to the kitchen, 'there's no need for you to stay on, Mrs. Telford. I'll fend for myself.'

When she had washed her hands Jocelyn went to the kitchen to find Mrs. Telford about to leave. A tray lay ready on the kitchen table and Mrs. Telford drew a covered plate from the oven as soon as she heard Jocelyn's footsteps and removed the lid to reveal a perfectly cooked mixed grill, steaming and appetizing. 'The dessert is in the fridge. I'll leave it there until you require it. Oh, and by the way, madam, a young man called. He said he was your brother. He waited for a while and then said he couldn't stay longer.'

Jocelyn froze. What could Alan have wanted? He had written her only a scrappy letter of thanks since Simon had settled his gambling debts. 'What time was he here, Mrs. Telford, and was he alone?'

'No, he had another young gentleman with him, and it must have been around five-thirty when he arrived. Yes, that's right, I remember hearing them listening to the news on the television while I was preparing your evening meal. They had the sound turned up rather high, I remember. It was about twenty minutes or so before he came into the kitchen and told me they wouldn't wait. I did suggest he telephone you at the office, Mrs. Wadebridge, or let me get them something to eat. They just had a whisky. I hope that was all right?'

As if in a dream Jocelyn nodded and as soon as she heard Mrs. Telford shut the front door she sped into the bedroom. Some premonition of disaster had already made her mouth go dry, and it was with the certainty that she would not find it that she looked on her dressing-table. The ring had gone – there was no doubt about it. In case she had misunderstood Mrs. Telford earlier Jocelyn even went into the bathroom, but that was clean and tidy, obviously having had its usual daily turn out. Jocelyn returned to search the drawers in her dressing-table, and it was then she discovered that the twenty pounds in cash she always kept for emergencies in her handkerchief drawer was also missing.

This would be the first place Alan would look, of course. Even as a little girl she had always kept her treasured possessions beneath her hankies, and it had been a household joke referred to by the Ashtead family as 'Jocelyn's safe'. She stood, both hands to her temples, her meal forgotten as she tried to decide what to do. It was then the bell rang and she hurried to throw open the front door, a hope bursting within her that Alan had thought better of his unlawful purloining of her property and had come back to return her ring at least.

But it was Neville Newton who stood outside, and catching a glimpse of her expression he came uninvited into the flat and closed the door behind him. 'What's the matter, Jocelyn?' then as she stared speechlessly at him, her mouth trembling, Neville pushed her into the living-room, saying, 'Come in here. What you need is a drink.'

He led her unresistingly to the nearest easy chair, poured out a stiff brandy and put it into her hand. 'Drink that! All of it,' as Jocelyn took a tentative sip, 'then you can tell me what's troubling you.'

Jocelyn obediently emptied the glass, gave a shudder as the undiluted spirit burned down her throat and handed the glass to Neville. 'Well?' he sounded patient but implacable.

'I've lost my engagement ring.'

Neville let out a gust of relieved laughter and turned to put down the glass. 'Is that all? I thought at the very least you'd found a body in the bathroom. Don't worry – Simon will get you another. And that reminds me, he phoned not long after you left to say they'd arrived safely and he hopes to be home on Wednesday. As I have to pass here on my way home I thought I'd call in and give you the message in person instead of telephoning. Good thing I did. You'd got yourself really worked up.'

Jocelyn moistened dry lips. She had no wish to tell Neville about her brother's misdemeanours. On the other hand, she had to ask someone's advice. 'I've had it stolen,' she blurted out baldly, 'by my brother or his friend.'

There was a second's astonished silence before Neville

drew up a chair and sat down beside her. 'Better tell me the whole story. It's all right,' he smiled slightly as Jocelyn looked up, shame in her eyes. 'Every family has its black sheep. How and when did the ring go missing?'

In disjointed sentences, interspersed by questions from Neville, Jocelyn told him the events leading up to her discovery of the missing money and ring. 'I *must* get it back. Simon will be absolutely furious when he finds out, but I can't tell the police. You must see that.'

Neville walked twice round the living-room, obviously deep in thought, while Jocelyn watched him anxiously. Suddenly he turned to her, saying as he did so, 'I see only three alternatives. Either you buy yourself an identical ring and leave it at that or you get someone to try to find out what those two young scoundrels have done with your ring. Or you can wait until Simon returns and let him handle it for you. Though it might be too late then to recover the ring. As it happens I was at school with a fellow who runs a detective agency with his father. No, don't look so apprehensive. They're nothing like the private eyes you see on television. Both Dick and his father have been in the police force and their integrity and reputation are beyond reproach. The only snag is their charges are pretty steep. Now what are you going to do?'

Jocelyn brushed her hair away from her forehead in a gesture which showed Neville plainly that she had quite lost her usual calm, unruffled manner and said, 'I don't know where Simon bought my ring. It was unusual and we could spend a week trying to find one like it. If Simon's returning on Wednesday we simply haven't time, and I don't want him to find out.'

'In that case the alternatives narrow down to one. I'll ring Dick, see if he can come over right away,' and without waiting to see Jocelyn's possible reactions Neville went over to the telephone.

Dick Walmer was nothing like Jocelyn's notion of a

private detective. For one thing he was elegant if not dandyish, in a perfectly tailored dark suit which he wore with a silk waistcoat of astonishingly vivid design. He was a little above average height and bone-thin, but Jocelyn felt a brief glimpse of hidden strength as he gripped her hand on being introduced.

He had a quiet and reassuring manner, so that recounting her brother's visit and the subsequent discovery of the missing money and ring did not turn out the ordeal Jocelyn had anticipated. Perhaps it was because of Dick's matter-of-fact manner. Neville had said he was an ex-policeman, so Dick had doubtless encountered too much crime, petty and otherwise, to be surprised at any of the stories clients poured into his receptive ears. 'Any idea where your brother and his friend were going when they left here?' he asked quietly when at last Jocelyn finished speaking.

'None at all. They won't have gone near the family, as my father doesn't approve of my brother's friend. We all think he's a bad influence on Alan.'

'Would they have gone to any of the friend's relatives, do you suppose?'

Jocelyn sighed. 'I've no idea if he had any. I think Christopher's parents are divorced and frankly I've never inquired about his personal life. Perhaps the boys have gone back to their flat in Leeds. They share with two other students.'

'Any chance of phoning them there?' and when Jocelyn shook her head, explaining there was no telephone in the flat, Dick Walmer nodded. 'Perhaps as well. If they are due back we don't want to tip our hand. Now you say your housekeeper let them in. If she's on the phone, ring and ask if she knows their plans for tonight.'

Mrs. Telford was obviously surprised to hear Jocelyn's voice, but there was no hesitation about her reply to the question. 'Your brother said they couldn't wait longer as they were on their way back to college. I remember distinctly because it made me wonder how they'd time to come to London during term. No offence meant, Mrs. Wadebridge.'

As she put the receiver back Jocelyn too wondered what Alan and Christopher had been doing away from lectures in the middle of term, but she kept this to herself as she reported Mrs. Telford's firm conviction that the two visitors had said they were on their way north. 'If that's true,' Dick Walmer said after a few moments' thought, 'the quicker we get up there the better. If we start now, we can be in Leeds by morning and they may not have had time to dispose of the ring before we reach them. Unless they know a market here in London for stolen jewellery. I'll just nip home, pack an overnight bag and have a word with my father. Can you be ready in, say, half an hour?' he asked Jocelyn.

Bemused by this rapid turn of events, Jocelyn could only nod. She was still standing, a dazed expression on her face, when Neville returned from letting Dick Walmer out. 'Come on, girl, look alive!' he prompted. 'You've nothing to worry about with Dick in charge. Should you need to stay over, I'll hold the fort at the office.'

Jocelyn smiled. It was a sorry effort, but all she could manage. 'Thanks, Neville, you're a dear.' She put out a hand and patted his arm affectionately as she passed to go to the bedroom. When she returned some fifteen minutes later, carrying a small zipped bag and a light coat over her arm, Neville was sitting sipping a whisky and soda and looking through some papers.

He got up as she entered and pointed to a plate of sandwiches and a steaming cup of coffee on the small table beside the settee. 'I saw you'd left your supper uneaten. You can't start a long journey with nothing inside you. Dick won't be here for another ten minutes, so get that down.'

Used to obeying Simon blindly, Jocelyn sat and began to nibble at one of the sandwiches. Now that everything had been taken so capably out of her hands she discovered she was hungry, and much to Neville's obvious satisfaction, by the time the front door bell shrilled again, her cup and plate were empty.

As he got up to answer the door Neville smiled, 'You'll do. Now don't worry. Leave everything to Dick.'

Looking back afterwards Jocelyn could never remember all the events of that journey. For the first hour, she and Dick chatted about his work, then the long road ahead, gleaming under a light drizzle, made Jocelyn's eyelids droop and she only awoke when the car stopped outside a transport café with the first fingers of dawn showing in the sky.

'Not far now,' Dick said as he leaned to unfasten first his own, then Jocelyn's safety belts. 'I don't know about you, but a hot meal wouldn't be unwelcome.'

Still only half awake as she was, there was nothing Jocelyn wanted less, but Dick gave her no chance to refuse. They were soon seated at a spotlessly clean table with plates of bacon, sausage and egg in front of them. Jocelyn watched fascinated as Dick picked up his knife and fork. He looked up, caught her eye and grinned. 'You'll find it's better than it looks. Dig in!'

Tea and toast would have been more to her taste, but Jocelyn did her best to do justice to the meal in front of her. Now the prospect of confronting Alan and Christopher loomed so close, it was with considerable difficulty that she swallowed only about a quarter of her plateful. To her immense relief Dick, who had eaten every scrap, made no comment. He lit a cigarette, ordered more coffee and sat looking replete and at ease.

He also looked to be deep in thought, but suddenly becoming aware of Jocelyn's eyes fixed upon his face, he stubbed out his cigarette. 'Something the matter?'

'I've suddenly got cold feet. Will there be trouble? I don't want anyone to get hurt.'

Dick Walmer laughed, though he looked a trifle sad.

'Oh dear, I wish the general public wouldn't always associate people in our profession with the deplorable image we're given on T.V. and the stage. In real life we don't do our work wearing dirty mackintoshes and knocking down everyone in sight. We try to carry out clients' wishes in as peaceful and unobtrusive a manner as possible. So for goodness' sake stop worrying. We're simply going to have a little talk with your brother and his friend. Nothing else, believe me.'

'No kung-fu?'

'No kung-fu,' Dick assured Jocelyn solemnly. 'Now shall we go?'

Jocelyn nodded and got to her feet, reassured by his sound common sense. Outside she stopped and drew a deep breath of the fresh early morning air. There were red streaks in the eastern sky, a warning of more rain to come, but for the moment it was fine and despite diesel fumes, after the hot atmosphere inside the café, the cool air felt fresh and pleasant. Jocelyn would liked to have lingered and delay the confrontation ahead, but Dick Walmer had unlocked the car and was holding the passenger door ready for her to climb in again.

Once in Leeds, they drove to one of the city's leading hotels where Dick arranged for Jocelyn to be given a room with a bath. 'You'll feel more like facing things when you've freshened up. Meet me downstairs in an hour. It's as well to be on the doorstep early in a case like this.'

The address of Alan Ashtead's flat was not difficult to find and an early milkman gave them detailed directions. What did prove difficult was trying to get an answer to their knock on the door. Dick Walmer hammered repeatedly before at last they heard the sound of footsteps and the door was swung open by a tousled young man who looked as if he had just fallen out of bed.

'Alan Ashtead. Is he here?' Jocelyn asked as the boy stood in silence holding the door, then as he did not answer she added, 'I'm his sister. Is he here? It's important.'

'Yes, he's here. Got in with Christopher about two a.m. They'll still be asleep. Couldn't it wait?'

'I'm afraid not. Mind if we come in?' Dick Walmer spoke for the first time and without waiting for an answer he pushed Jocelyn over the threshhold and closed the door. 'Where does Alan sleep? Show us, then you can go back to bed. We're sorry to have disturbed you.'

'That's their room,' the boy who had admitted them pointed towards a closed door at the end of the hall. 'Help yourself, but for heaven's sake be quiet. We had a bit of a party last night. I didn't intend to get up till noon,' and he vanished into his own room.

Dick Walmer gave Jocelyn a reassuring grin before he quietly opened Alan's bedroom door and they entered the darkened room. As he drew the curtains aside and daylight flooded into the room, a figure in the nearest bed groaned and Jocelyn recognized her brother. He opened his eyes and stared as if she were a ghost, then sat up to ask, 'How did you get here? And who's that with you?'

Jocelyn answered neither question as she crossed to the bedside. 'How could you, Alan! Oh, not the money – that didn't matter. But my ring. How could you take my ring? I suppose Mrs. Telford told you Simon was away and you couldn't resist the temptation to take a rise out of him.'

Alan's face had been showing more and more amazement as her almost incoherent speech proceeded. 'Slow down, Sis. I can't make head or tail of what you're going on about. Sure I took some money. I knew you'd let me have it had you been home. But a ring! I know nothing about any ring.'

Despite her past experience of Alan, this assertion had a note of sincerity about it, and Jocelyn looked across at Dick in some bewilderment. Then enlightenment dawned as she suddenly noticed that the figure in the other bed was remarkably still even for someone deeply asleep after a late night.

Dick Walmer's eyes followed her own. He walked briskly across to Christopher Tenby's bed and twitched aside the bedclothes. 'I think you heard what Mrs. Wadebridge was saying to her brother. Where's the ring you took from her flat last night?'

'Try and find out.' Christopher's voice was defiant.

'Don't worry, I will. Jocelyn, take your brother into the kitchen. Make him a cup of tea. I'd like a word or two alone with this young man.'

It took Jocelyn some time to persuade Alan to leave Christopher and Dick Walmer alone, but at last, clad in a towelling dressing-gown, he reluctantly led the way to the kitchen where he slumped down at the table as Jocelyn filled the kettle and put it on the gas to boil. The sink was filled with dirty dishes, but she managed to wash and wipe three mugs, find enough fresh milk for tea and a bag of sugar. By the time Dick Walmer sauntered into the kitchen the tea was made and Jocelyn was giving it a few minutes to brew.

She looked up, anxiety in her face, but Dick's expression revealed little. He drew out a chair and sat down at the table facing Alan as Jocelyn poured the tea with a shaking hand.

There was silence as Dick stirred sugar into his mug and Jocelyn glanced from his impassive face to that of her brother's. At last Dick spoke. 'Your friend had ninety-seven pounds,' he stopped to scatter a roll of notes and some coins on the table, 'and precisely seventy-two pence in his pockets. Is he usually so flush?'

Alan looked sulky, but at last mumbled 'No' in answer to Dick's question.

'Did you come up here by train last night?' Alan looked surprised at the sudden alteration in Dick's line of inquiry, but this time he replied without hesitation. 'No, we hitched.'

'And did you stop anywhere between the time you left

your sister's flat and making for Leeds?'

Alan began to look sulky again until Dick went on, 'You may as well tell me. I believe you when you say you had nothing to do with the theft of the ring, but I intend getting it back. Your friend apparently got a hundred for it. Now did you stop anywhere before hitching back?'

In his neat suit and showy waistcoat he did not look to Jocelyn particularly formidable, but apparently Dick Walmer's fashionable appearance did not fool Alan. Sensing the toughness and determination behind the easygoing façade, he said sullenly, 'We stopped at a pub for a drink, that's all.'

'Speak to anyone there?'

'Only the landlord when Christopher bought the drinks.'

'And the name of the pub?'

Alan gave the name and location, whereupon a beatific smile spread over Dick's features and he let out a satisfied 'Ah!' Downing the rest of his tea, he got to his feet, picked up the roll of notes and said to Jocelyn, 'Come on, let's get going, Mrs. Wadebridge.' He turned to Alan. 'Tell your friend he may keep the seventy-two pence and that this is his first and only reprieve. If he so much as sets foot near Mrs. Wadebridge in the future it will be a police matter next time.'

Jocelyn followed him to the door, but there she stopped and turned to face her young brother. 'Get Christopher Tenby off your back, Alan, please. He's going to lead you into real trouble one of these days.'

Dick Walmer drove them back in silence to the hotel where he and Jocelyn had stayed earlier. As he opened the passenger door of the car he said consolingly, 'There's nothing more you can do for the moment, so go and lie down until lunchtime. I've a phone call to make, then I intend putting my own feet up for a couple of hours. Meet me down here, say,' he glanced at his watch, 'one-fifteen. We'll have a meal and drive back to London this afternoon.'

'But my ring . . .'

'Leave that to me. I reckon we'll have it back by tomorrow if not before.'

There was nothing to do but take his advice. Jocelyn walked towards the lift as Dick went across the foyer towards the public telephone booth. Once in the impersonal bedroom upstairs, she slipped off her top garments, washed, and slid under the eiderdown, sure she would never sleep after the anxiety of the past twelve hours. Nature thought otherwise and only the clatter of a dustbin lid being dropped in the street outside awoke her shortly before it was time to get up, dress and go down to meet Dick.

Conversation flagged on the journey back to London, Dick intent on the concentration of driving and Jocelyn lost in miserable contemplation of Alan's latest escapade. She roused herself to offer to share the driving, but a sideways glance at her companion's face made her see that such a suggestion would be turned down out of hand.

In his way, Jocelyn thought, and a small wry smile just touched the corners of her mouth, Dick Walmer was as unapproachable and aloof as Simon himself. He would no doubt laugh at her solicitude in thinking him incapable of having the resilience to do this trip twice in such a short time. Certainly his face revealed no sign of strain, and as if sensing Jocelyn's mixed-up thoughts, he shot her a sideways glance and smiled. 'We'll soon be home now, and if I know anything about my father he'll have located your ring.'

He was right. Driving direct to the small unobtrusive offices from which the detective agency was run, Jocelyn was introduced to Dick's father, a larger and older edition of his son and with the same calm assurance about him. After seeing Jocelyn to a chair, he opened a drawer in his desk, took out an envelope and pushed it across.

As she pulled out her engagement ring Jocelyn released a sigh of relief which made the two men smile. 'You had no trouble, then?' Dick asked as Jocelyn slid the ring thankfully on to her finger.

'None at all,' Dick's father replied at once, 'but then our man knew he'd be well paid with no danger of tangling with the law. You see, Mrs. Wadebridge,' Mr. Walmer said, turning to Jocelyn, 'to keep the matter quiet as you requested, I'm afraid I had to pay handsomely to recover your ring; though it goes against the grain to let these villains get away with it,' he finished.

'I can't thank you enough,' Jocelyn got to her feet. 'Please let me know what I owe you.'

Dick Walmer took her arm. 'Don't worry now. We'll send you our account by post. Meantime let me run you home.'

Next morning when Jocelyn went to consult Neville over some decisions that needed his agreement he looked at her left hand and asked, 'Dick Walmer solve your problem? Yes, I can see he did.'

'Thank you for introducing him. I'd never have recovered the ring on my own.' Jocelyn hesitated for a moment, disliking what she had to add. 'You won't mention my stupidity to Simon, will you, Neville? He might not understand why I simply didn't call the police when I discovered the ring was gone.'

Neville didn't answer for a moment, his eyes on Jocelyn's flushed unhappy face. 'I think you underestimate Simon, but if you want me to keep the whole business under wraps, of course I will,' and muttering almost incoherent words of gratitude, Jocelyn whisked herself out of the office and went back to her own, wishing she did not feel so guilty at involving Neville.

There had been no word from Simon about the date of his return, and the following evening, bored with her own company, Jocelyn decided to have a bath and an early night. She was just about to step into the hot water as the telephone rang, and grabbing a dressing-gown she hurried to answer, hoping it was a message from Simon.

Immediately she recognized her brother's voice, and sensed more trouble. 'You remember telling me to get Christopher off my back, Jocelyn?' Alan asked, then without waiting for an answer he went on, 'You might have saved yourself the trouble. He cleared out this morning while the rest of us were attending a lecture and he's taken everything of value he could turn into cash as well as the rent and housekeeping money we'd put by for the remainder of term. Can you send me fifty pounds?'

Jocelyn was stunned into silence by Alan's sheer effrontery, until his voice in her ear said, 'Jocelyn! Are you still there?'

'Yes, I'm here. I suppose it's not much to pay to see the back of him.'

'That's not what the other chaps think, and they blame me for introducing Chris. Can you send the money right away? I tried to get an advance from the college bursar, but he wouldn't play. I'm sorry. I expect the other business cost you plenty.' His young voice sounded contrite.

'You can say that again!' Jocelyn replied, a grim note in her own voice as she thought of the bill from the Walmer Detective Agency lying in her handbag. It would put her account at the bank badly in the red when she paid it, without the extra worry of finding an additional fifty pounds for Alan. The obvious course would be to tell Simon all about it on his return, but his opinion of Alan was low enough already without her having to confess her brother's latest predicament. The actual theft of the ring had not been any of his doing, nevertheless Jocelyn could visualize Simon's reaction were she to confess the whole unpleasant episode. Later when she went down to post the cheque Jocelyn hoped Alan had learnt his lesson, because this was the last time, she vowed to herself, she would help him out of a jam.

CHAPTER FIVE

SHE slept fitfully during the first part of the night chased by nightmares, then in the small hours fell into a deep sleep, dreaming she was in Simon's arms kissing and being kissed in return. She awoke to find him sitting on the bed beside her, laughing as she opened her eyes wide in amazement.

'How on earth did you get here?' Even as she uttered the words Jocelyn was wondering what if any of her dream had been real. Had Simon been kissing her in fact just before she awoke, and if so what could he be thinking, for in her dream she had been kissing him passionately in return.

She flushed under his amused gaze as he replied, 'Took you unawares, didn't I? As a matter of fact I got the chance of a flight yesterday evening and decided to surprise you.'

He got to his feet and taking off his jacket hung it over the back of a chair. 'I'll be glad to get out of my things and into a bath, but tea first, eh? I've got the kettle on. It should be boiling by this time.'

He was back in five minutes with two cups on a small tray and Jocelyn sat up to enjoy the unexpected pleasure of his company. She blinked as he sat down again, hardly able to realize he was here in the flesh, and watched with fascinated eyes as he picked up her hand and played with her rings for a moment before looking up to catch her eye and say softly, 'Miss me, Kitten?'

Apparently he did not expect a reply, for he turned her hand to press a kiss on the palm and with a grave face fold her fingers over the place his lips had touched. 'I must get out of these filthy clothes,' he suddenly announced. 'Hold on to this,' and he laid her closed hand on the quilt.

A glance at her bedside clock showed Jocelyn it was barely six-thirty, and her lips curled into a smile of pure contentment as Simon's voice singing the theme song from a recent film reached her from the bathroom. She drained her cup and snuggled back on to the pillows. It was certainly nice to have a man about the place again. One got used to having someone solid to rely on. Then Jocelyn's smile faded as niggling thoughts of the events of the last few days dimmed the excitement of Simon's unexpected early return. There would be an all too familiar frown in his eyes if he got to hear of Alan's latest débâcle and she had no wish to dispel the mood he was in for it was all too rare.

When Simon returned clad in a towelling bathrobe, his hair still damp from the shower, there seemed an air of suppressed excitement about him which prompted Jocelyn to say, 'You're looking specially pleased with yourself. Did you arrange something profitable when you were in New York?'

Simon sat down again on the bed, idly rubbing his hair with a small towel. 'Are you suggesting I only look happy when I've pulled off an advantageous deal? Might my joie-de-vivre not be for the sheer pleasure of being home again, Kitten? You seemed as delighted as me that I came home earlier than expected. *Before* you opened your eyes, that is. I hope you don't kiss every man who comes into your bedroom so enthusiastically!'

Jocelyn's face turned a bright pink at these words. So she had *not* entirely dreamed that masterful embrace nor the demanding lips which had claimed her own – but how typical of Simon to make fun of it, to turn the incident into something to be laughed at rather than cherished. She could feel the all too familiar lump in her throat as she willed the flush to die down. Would nothing ever penetrate his indifference to her feelings? Pulling on a dressing gown, she decided for once to answer back.

'Not every man,' she replied, amazed at her own daring, 'only a favoured half dozen or so.'

As she walked past him, Simon laughed and caught her by the wrist. 'I really believe at long last you're cutting your wisdom teeth, Kitten. Good for you!' and releasing her, he got up to go over to the dressing table and begin to brush his hair. Jocelyn eyed his back for a few seconds with rising indignation. She might have known he would turn her remark aside as being of no account, she thought, as she made for the bathroom door. Tears of anger were almost blinding her as she turned on the shower, then removing dressing gown and nightdress, stood under the water until her anger had cooled.

As she towelled herself she suddenly remembered Simon's last remark. He didn't believe her capable of being unfaithful for a second, yet he hadn't sounded displeased at her unusual impudence. Three months ago she would never have dreamed of speaking to him in such a fashion and had often envied the verbal fencing which came so easily to some. Perhaps, unnoticed by herself, at last she was learning self-confidence. She went to get dressed, for once careless of Simon's reactions and found him some ten minutes later in the kitchen cheerfully preparing their breakfast. He put a glass of fresh orange juice in front of her before turning to supervise the sizzling rashers under the grill.

He was humming the same tune he had been singing in his shower and as she sipped Jocelyn chided herself for finding such pleasure in merely sharing a breakfast table with this man. She was beginning to understand why so many of the females with whom he came in contact fell victim to his charm, for like the bubbles in champagne, excitement she was incapable of controlling was beginning to well up inside. Determined to get her feet safely back on terra firma, Jocelyn looked up as Simon pulled out his chair and began to eat. 'I expect you'll be wanting a report on things at the agency before we go in.'

Simon looked up and Jocelyn noticed for the first time his casual clothes, for he hadn't dressed in the usual formal lounge suit he normally wore for the office. 'Now why should you think that? I'm sure you and Neville have coped admirably.' His voice hardened. 'I'd hardly have left you had I not thought so.'

He hesitated a moment as he reached for another slice of toast before he looked across at Jocelyn and with what looked remarkably like deliberate persuasion in his voice asked, 'Wouldn't you like to take a couple of days off? I know I would, and if we've to be in Wales on Saturday for the week-end we could motor there at our leisure. How about it?'

'Wales?' Jocelyn's voice squeaked with surprise and Simon's smile faded, to be replaced by his dismaying frown. 'Yes, you surely can't have forgotten. The Pendleton child. The christening is on Sunday.'

Jocelyn put a hand to her head and Simon's voice dropped to almost a murmur. 'It's not like you to forget a thing like that, Kitten. Something happen to upset you?'

She looked up. 'Of course not.' She wished her voice would not wobble when Simon fixed her with that searching questioning look. 'We've been busy and I guess it just slipped my memory.'

Simon looked away to pick up the coffee pot and refill their cups and Jocelyn let out a small sigh of relief that the shrewd eyes were no longer fixed on her face. 'So you haven't remembered to buy the napkin ring you fancied either, nor arranged to have it engraved?' His tones were still a mere murmur and as Jocelyn shook her head he pushed back his chair to go and fetch a cigarette.

To her astonishment he did no more questioning, simply saying as he sat down again and stirred sugar into his coffee, 'Never mind. You get off to the office. I'll see to the christening present and be in later.'

When Jocelyn was ready to leave she found Simon

hidden behind a newspaper and as she hesitated, at a loss, he peered over the top of the paper and gave her one of his all-encompassing glances. Suddenly to her surprise his eyes began to twinkle and he lowered the paper further to say, 'You should wear that particular shade of peacock green more often. And I like the shoes. New?'

Jocelyn glanced down at her slim legs and the new black court shoes. 'Yes, they're the latest from Italy. I was extravagant and got two pairs.'

'They certainly do things for a girl's legs. Seems a shame to waste them on the office. Shall I book a table for lunch?'

Jocelyn studied the smiling grey eyes. It was so difficult to know these days when Simon was serious or otherwise. It increased if anything her feeling of walking on quicksands, and she retorted impulsively, 'Book a table if you like, but what makes you think my shoes will go unnoticed at the office? We don't run a nunnery, and anyway, I have an appointment this afternoon with the representative from *Elle* magazine. Do you think he'll approve too?'

'Not a doubt of it.' Jocelyn looked up from shrugging into a lightweight black coat to find that somehow or other in that short interval Simon had got up and was between her and the outer door. 'Aren't you going to kiss me goodbye?' he asked mockingly.

She blinked, more from surprise than fright. 'But it will smudge my make-up.'

It was the first reaction which popped into her mind. Left to herself, she made do with the merest hint of lipstick and a little soft eye-shadow, but Mrs. Wadebridge had always insisted on the full treatment for business, though Jocelyn drew the line at false eyelashes.

'So it might.' Simon was still between her and the door, but the mocking look had gone out of his eyes and he looked merely amused. 'Don't you consider it worth a smudge or two to say goodbye properly?'

'I'll be late if I don't go now,' Jocelyn went on, ignoring his question.

'Hasn't it occurred to you yet that occasionally it does people no harm to be kept waiting?' he asked, and her eyes widened in startled surprise.

'But you hate unpunctuality. You've always said it's the ultimate in discourtesy.'

'In business, yes. For social occasions unpunctuality in a woman is expected. Indeed it often whets the appetite.' Then, taking pity on her obvious confusion at this astounding piece of advice, Simon stood aside. 'Off you go, then, Kitten. Don't look so worried. Everything works out in the end.'

Walking briskly to the agency, Jocelyn could make no sense of Simon's strange behaviour. He was being puzzling in the extreme and she could think of no reason to account for his unaccustomed good humour. He could be kind and understanding as well as autocratic and uncompromising, but this was the first time he had behaved towards her in so human and approachable a manner.

The morning at the agency passed with more than its accustomed systematic programme of interviews, correspondence and calls, so that Jocelyn was surprised when Gwenda put her head round the door and announced that as Anne had returned she and Fay were going to lunch together. A glance at her wristwatch showed that it was nearly one-thirty. Where could Simon have got to? He was certainly showing a most unusual lack of interest in his beloved business.

If she were to keep her three o'clock appointment Jocelyn knew she must go and have a snack right away. As she went through the reception area, Anne at her desk looked up and hastily pushed a newspaper into her top drawer, wearing a real 'caught in the act' look, Jocelyn thought as she pushed open the glass entrance door. Before she went in to order a coffee and sandwich in the nearby serve-yourself café, she purchased an early edition of the evening paper and spread it open.

She didn't have to look far to find what had captured Anne's interest. There on the front page was an unmistakable likeness of Candida Melbourne, her hand tucked possessively into Simon's, and underneath the information that 'top model and cover girl Candida Melbourne had arrived back in London to star in a new T.V. series due to start rehearsal'. No wonder Simon had sung in his shower and looked as if Ernie had just handed him a top prize! His reluctance to come to the office too. Now it all slotted neatly into place and Jocelyn, even while amazement at her own blindness overwhelmed her, felt anger churning inside.

What an idiot they must think her! How conveniently docile and manageable! Jocelyn, her teeth clenched, deliberately let the newspaper slide to the floor, ignoring the astonishment in the eyes of the housewife opposite, who stooped to retrieve it. She just managed a hasty 'thank you' as she got up, snatching at handbag and newspaper to hurry out into the busy street.

By the time she reached the agency her anger, instead of cooling during the fight through pedestrian-crowded pavements, had reached boiling point. Anne, still alone in Reception, looked up as Jocelyn hurried in and her eyes widened at the poppy-red cheeks. 'Simon arrived just after you left. Said he'd like a word as soon as you returned from lunch.'

Wanted a word, did he? Jocelyn thought bitterly as she stalked through her old office and entered Simon's. He was sitting at his desk and remained so as she threw the newspaper down in front of him and burst out, 'And to think I wondered why you returned this morning so full of the joy of living! The trouble with you is you want your cake and your ha'penny as well. I hate you! I've a very good mind to walk right out here and now and leave you to stew in your own juice!'

Jocelyn stopped, partly because there were so many

past injustices she wanted to throw in Simon's face and for the life of her she couldn't summon a specific instance to mind on the spur of the moment.

'You won't, you know,' Simon's reply to her gauntlet was dangerously quiet.

'Why shouldn't I?' Jocelyn, usually inarticulate in Simon's presence, heard herself retort. 'You may not mind sniggers at my expense all over the office, but I can assure you I do!'

Simon came round the desk to face her and he was smiling infuriatingly as if at a fractious child who needed coaxing to heel. 'Now, Kitten, simmer down. No one's laughing at you.'

'And don't call me Kitten!' Jocelyn shouted, her self-control for once in danger of slipping completely. 'Do you and Candida expect me to sit back, smile and condone an affair carried on right under my nose? It was different before we were married, but you surely didn't expect to carry on as before. Or perhaps you actually did!'

She turned away, her outburst fizzling to a stop like a damp squib. Iron hands turned her back and she was forced to meet the steely gaze which inevitably reduced her to a jelly. 'I am not, repeat not, carrying on right under your nose – or anywhere else come to that.' Simon's lips hardly moved, yet the enunciation was clear and distinct. 'And you are not walking out, now or ever! Understand? We've never gone in for divorce in my family or even separation, and I'm not about to create a precedent. You are my wife and my wife you'll stay, like it or not. And at the week-end we shall go down to Wales where you will give the Pendletons every reason to suppose that we're a devoted couple. And you will give as well as receive. Understand?'

Jocelyn did understand, and her humiliated stare revealed as much. The hands shook her quite sharply. 'As well as receiving my embraces as if they were welcome you will occasionally give me a passing caress uninvited –

like any other newlywed bride who can hardly bear to keep her hands off her ever-loving husband,' Simon went on, then as Jocelyn flushed and shrank between his hands, the grip tightened and he said harshly, 'Angie Pendleton is a nice girl, an intelligent one. I wouldn't want her even to suspect everything wasn't perfect in our private garden and spoil the atmosphere at Philip's christening. She's done you the honour of asking you to sponsor him, after all, and in her book that's no light mark of esteem.'

Jocelyn's brief revolt had burned itself out minutes ago and she merely nodded. Apparently satisfied that she would as usual obey without argument, Simon released her, saying as she did so, 'By the way, I hope you haven't made any arrangements for tonight. We'll dine at home.'

Jocelyn, sheer hopelessness keeping her silent, turned to the door, thankful that Gwenda fortunately was still at lunch. Using the door which led into the rear corridor, she let herself into her own office, glad she could avoid Reception by this private route. It was unlikely that anyone could have overheard the head-on clash with Simon, but Jocelyn needed a few minutes to re-do her make-up and try to control her shaking limbs before she faced anyone.

She could not, however, have quite regained her usual air of calm, for Neville, coming in to join her for the three o'clock appointment, asked, 'Feeling all right, Jo? You're looking a bit green.' Jocelyn just had time to say, 'I think I may have eaten something at lunch which didn't agree with me,' when Anne came in to announce their visitor.

'Swallowed' would have been nearer the truth, Jocelyn thought privately as she automatically introduced the two men, for it had been a bitter pill to discover the real reason for Simon's early return home and unusual geniality. Oh, how wonderful to have that 'certain something' which apparently Candida possessed. What the French described as a bit of *je ne sais quoi*. It was more than beauty, more subtle than self-assurance. Jocelyn felt she must be destined to miss the boat where the Simons of this world were concerned, for more than a fair share of disappointment seemed to come her way.

The evening should have been fraught with tension, the last ripples of their quarrel still lingering in the air, but Simon seemed to have put the whole episode out of his mind. He was his usual baffling, non-committal self, making Mrs. Telford blush with pleasure at a souvenir he had brought back for her and Jocelyn angry by saying casually, 'By the way, Mother sent you something to wear. It's all the rage in America for evenings at home. Go and put it on.'

Still managing me, even from three thousand miles away! Jocelyn thought resentfully as she went to do his bidding, but when she returned clad in the heavy Japanese silk housecoat she was careful not to let any sign of her ingratitude show. As they sat down to eat she asked lightly, 'How was your mother?'

'Very much the American matron. You'd never guess she'd done anything in her life except play bridge and give coffee mornings. The only sign of her obsessive passion for organization that I could see was that already she's on umpteen committees.'

Despite a heavy heart Jocelyn found herself laughing at this last snippet of information. 'Dare I say, America beware?'

Simon laughed too as he leaned forward to pour out the wine and the stern autocrat of this afternoon had disappeared for the moment. 'You may, and it should. Talking of families, Margaret phoned just after you left this morning – wanted us to go over there for supper. I told them it was time she and Jack came here. We'll have an early meal tomorrow and take them to a theatre. I've already warned Mrs. Telford there'll be four for supper and booked seats, so there's nothing for you to bother about.'

Jocelyn wiped her lips with her napkin and mumbled, 'Thanks.' Was this Simon's way of smoothing over the cracks? A family party certainly would give the lie to the implication behind the photograph in this afternoon's newspaper. It seemed hardly possible, but he might even be wary of her father's reactions should he see the photograph.

The following evening as they were about to leave for the theatre, the telephone rang. Jocelyn answered to hear Pablo Pendleton's unmistakable voice say, 'I rang to check about the week-end, Jo. We're just off. Am I to tell Mother to expect you on Saturday?'

Simon, who had been helping Margaret Ashstead into her coat, came over to take the receiver out of Jocelyn's hand. He had obviously realized the drift of the conversation, for he said without preamble, 'Pablo! I meant to give you a ring, sorry! Jocelyn and I intend coming to Wales by easy stages, so will some time late Saturday be convenient?' Apparently the reply was in the affirmative, for after a few more laughing exchanges Simon put down the phone.

More dictatorial decisions, Jocelyn thought rebelliously as she went to join her father and stepmother, though to do Simon justice, she had already admitted that the christening had completely slipped her memory. Just the same, he might have asked her opinion. For all he knew, she might not want to go to Wales 'by easy stages', whatever that might mean, but at least it ruled out a rendezvous with Candida Melbourne. Even Simon could not be in two places at once.

But next day Jocelyn found that she had underestimated Candida's hold on Simon's attention. She was tidying her desk and wondering if Simon was going to suggest they had a bar lunch at the local when he strolled into her office. 'Candida just phoned. I'm taking her to lunch,' he announced baldly, then as Jocelyn's lips visibly tightened he smiled sardonically. 'You look quite murderous, Kitten. Wouldn't be a fraction dog-in-the-mangerish, would you? After all, it can't be jealousy. You have to be in love to experience that.'

There was a gleam of pure devilry in his eyes as Jocelyn said sharply, 'I asked you not to call me Kitten! I find it most distasteful.'

His hand on the door handle, Simon turned and she saw his lips part in an even more mocking smile. 'Sorry, Kitten, I'll try to remember. By the way, I rang and asked Mrs. Telford to pack our things for the week-end and I'll be picking the bags up some time during the afternoon, so we can get away as soon as the office closes. Neville and Walter will hold the fort tomorrow.'

As the door closed, Jocelyn sank weakly into her chair and stared blankly through the window. Neville Newton, coming in, brought her abruptly back to her surroundings. 'Simon's got stuck with Candida for a press luncheon, so how about having a bite with me?' he invited, and nodding gratefully, Jocelyn got up and collected her handbag. So that was the reason for the lunch. Why couldn't Simon have told her? Apparently she was the last these days to hear of her own husband's appointments. She had been more 'in the picture' when merely his secretary, she thought wryly, as Neville held open the outer door to let her pass.

Easing their way out of London through the homegoing commuters augmented this evening by week-enders like themselves, Jocelyn and Simon were both silent, he intent on driving and she still dismally aware that he had not returned from the lunch date with Candida until nearly five o'clock. Even taking into consideration his detour to collect their suitcases, it must have been a very protracted press session, and Jocelyn's ego felt even more flattened by the fact that Simon had not bothered to tell her of his movements since one o'clock. If she summoned up the necessary courage to ask where he had been he would undoubtedly give her one of his calculated snubs –

or worse, treat her questioning with the mixture of bland provocation and teasing which she found so infuriating.

He had obviously decided to ignore their earlier hassle, for when London was safely behind them he turned to meet Jocelyn's moody stare. Ignoring the resentment in her eyes, he said, 'Well, we made it. I know a good hotel the other side of Reading where we can stop and have dinner. Then you can decide where you'd like to spend the night. There are a couple of alternatives. We can take our pick because they're holding a room at both. I intend to take things easy for the next couple of days. America is stimulating, but give me the English countryside every time for real relaxation.'

Jocelyn had been fully determined to remain aloof, a little on her dignity. But how could any girl, she asked herself, keep her distance when eyes more usually quelling than reassuring looked into hers with such disarming consideration or when her fingers were being caressed by a gentle thumb?

She let out an audible sigh and Simon lifted her hand, gave it a kiss and returned it to her lap. 'Not to worry, Pussy-cat. Things will work out. Give them time.'

Yes, they would work out, Jocelyn thought, and tried to feel resigned as her fingers still tingled from his touch. But work out how? And for whose benefit? She supposed as Simon's wife she had a certain status, though it was small comfort. Candida with her beauty and sophisticated experience held all the trump cards. There was nothing Jocelyn could do but soldier on philosophically and Simon was certainly making this easy at the moment. But for how long would his mellow mood last?

They stopped for dinner at a riverside hotel in rural countryside, and as it was a particularly mild evening, took their coffee at a table in the garden set beside the river. One or two launches were still afloat, possibly on their way to nearby moorings, for the children on one which passed close in to the bank were already in pyjamas. Jocelyn waved as they passed and turned to find Simon watching.

The smile faded slowly from her lips as their eyes locked. She felt like a trapped rabbit unable to look away from the grey eyes summing up the immediate apprehension in her own. But there was nothing alarming in his soft, easy drawl as he asked, 'Why are you still so afraid of me? No ...' he continued as Jocelyn instinctively began to shake her head in denial, 'it's no use denying it. For some reason half the time you're like a cat on hot bricks when I'm about. For the life of me I can't think why. To look at you now, anyone would suppose I was about to beat you. Perhaps it might be an idea,' he continued pensively and let his eyes slide away as he reached for the coffeepot and refilled their cups. 'You know what they say about "a woman, a spaniel and a walnut tree"?'

Jocelyn smiled and willed herself to sound relaxed as she answered. 'Of course. "The more you beat them the better they be." But you've no need of a whip or a sword, your tongue is weapon enough. Isn't it supposed to be mightier than the sword?'

'No, my sweet ignoramus. It's the pen that's mightier. You think I beat you with words, then?'

'Yes, but then of course I'm not beautiful or celebrated, nor about to make a T.V. series,' Jocelyn finished with a bitter note in her voice.

'I take it we're back to Candida?' the tones were silky now and danger threatened. Maybe it was the advancing twilight that gave Jocelyn courage to finish the conversation instead of relapsing into sulky silence.

'Well, isn't it a fact that at the moment she's top of your hit parade? Though I've not forgotten her predecessors.'

To her astonishment Simon burst into a shout of laughter which made others enjoying the amenities of the riverside hotel turn and stare. 'Did you really expect me to live the life of a hermit while I waited for the right moment to settle down? If you did you've still a lot to learn about men, my sweet.'

Jocelyn did not contradict Simon's last statement. Rather she would have said she had everything to learn about men. Did one ever become accustomed to the way their minds worked? she wondered as she added cream to the cooling coffee in her cup. Simon in many ways was as much an enigma as the day she had first gone to work for him, a gauche awkward teenager learning to live in an adult world without a mother to turn to for advice. Had he realized how difficult life might be settling down with a stepmother, however pleasant that stepmother might be? Perhaps he had, in which case the job which had cropped up so opportunely might not have been offered by chance.

She glanced at Simon to find he was smoking quietly and watching the river glinting in the lights reflected from the building at their backs. As if aware of her regard, he turned and smiled. 'Finished your coffee? What's it to be, then? Do we stop here for the night or push on for an hour or so to a nice little place about fifty miles further north?'

It seemed the earlier conversation and its discomfiting questions had been put in mothballs, but Simon would resurrect it at some future date, Jocelyn felt sure. 'Let's push on. I don't know about you, but after that huge meal I've no desire to go to bed yet. It's put new life into me.'

If Simon imagined she was employing delaying tactics he gave no sign. 'I'm glad you're feeling better. You were looking tired when we arrived.' He didn't miss a trick, Jocelyn thought as they walked out to the car. Living with Simon was like living under a microscope. He missed nothing.

The 'nice little place' was more than nice, it was delightful. Genuine old beams met Jocelyn's delighted inspection when Simon left her in the cosy bar to inquire about their room, and she was soon deep in conversation with a rotund old gentleman of some eighty summers who was occupying the obvious seat of privilege beside the empty fireplace, on this warm summer evening holding a charming arrangement of flowers instead of a fire. Simon looked amused as Jocelyn introduced him as 'my husband', and the old man, delighted to have his audience increased by one, gladly accepted Simon's offer of a pint.

He seemed to know everyone within a radius of ten miles, having been born and brought up in a cottage 'pace or two down the road'. 'That can mean anything from five minutes' walk to a couple of miles around here,' Simon whispered as one of the old man's cronies called a greeting across the bar. 'Come on, say good night to your elderly admirer. You look ready to fall asleep in your chair.'

'I am feeling sleepy now,' Jocelyn admitted as Simon pulled out her chair and they said good night to their companion. His bright eyes followed them and when they were climbing the uncarpeted oak staircase leading to the upper floor Simon said, 'The old boy took a real shine to you. I can see it's not safe to leave you alone. A good thing none of the village Casanovas were in tonight.'

'You flatter me,' Jocelyn said as they reached the upper landing. 'I think the prospect of a free drink was a good deal more irresistible than my sex appeal,' then as Simon opened the door marked with a shiny figure five she exclaimed, 'Goodness, we've got a double bed – a fourposter too!'

Simon put down their bags, revealing little surprise. 'Probably repro, though, because it's got a spring interior mattress, heaven be praised.'

'You've been here before.' It was a statement more than a question and at Simon's smiling nod Jocelyn asked sharply, 'Alone?'

Simon looked down to regard her with curiosity in his usually unfathomable grey eyes. 'You must be joking, dear girl.' Jocelyn turned her head away, aware that she should have known better than ask such a leading question, since she had only laid herself open to yet another of Simon's hurtful setdowns. Suddenly he reached out and took her by the chin, turning her unwilling face until their glances met. 'With Mother,' he explained, pinching her chin before releasing her to unlock their cases. 'The bathroom's right next door. You go first.'

Wordlessly, Jocelyn got out nightdress, dressing-gown and slippers, and collected her sponge bag before she let herself out into the corridor. When she returned some thirty minutes later Simon was sitting in the only armchair the room boasted reading through some documents, and he looked up as Jocelyn slipped off her dressing-gown to turn back the bedclothes.

His eyes crinkled at the corners. 'In that nightie you only need a frilly nightcap and you might be straight out of *David Copperfield*. It suits you,' he finished, taking the sting out of the casual comment.

As she climbed into the high bed Jocelyn couldn't help a sensation of pure pleasure steal over her at the unlooked-for compliment. Despite its old-fashioned style, the turquoise nightdress with its white lace edging at neck and hem was a bit of feminine nonsense to which she had succumbed in a fit of extravagance one lunchtime, since she normally wore sensible pyjamas.

Jocelyn awoke with a start next morning, disturbed by unaccustomed bird-song right outside the window. She lay for some minutes trying to orientate herself, then opening her eyes immediately recognized her surroundings. The bedside clock pointed to seven-thirty, which meant early tea would be coming soon. Moving cautiously, she turned to look at Simon, who was to all intents and purposes fast asleep.

Jocelyn, now wide awake, could not resist the opportunity of examining his face in detail at such close quarters. He was lying on his back with his face towards her and slowly she let her eyes drift down from the bronzed forehead, the straight dark brows, the thick lashes and straight nose to his mouth.

Here her gaze lingered as she wished she were clever enough to figure him out. Those firm lips had issued orders, delivered reprimands, even roused her to physical ardour, yet she was no nearer to understanding their owner. Suddenly she jumped as one corner of his mouth twitched and hardly moving his lips he murmured, 'Go on, be a devil. Kiss me if you want to.'

She had been so engrossed she had not noticed he was peeping at her between narrowed lids. She was about to accuse him of unfair play when a knock came on the bedroom door and she heard the sound of crockery rattling. She hastily turned her head into the pillow and pretended to be asleep, not even stirring when Simon thanked the maid, asked her to put the tray his side and returned her, 'It's going to be another lovely day' with, 'Yes, so it would seem.'

'Coward!' he remarked lazily as the door closed again and Jocelyn raised a face pink with embarrassment. 'Afraid she might think we're a honeymoon couple or maybe even on a sly week-end if she'd come in and found us kissing? Shame on you! I thought you'd more pluck.'

Enough was enough, Jocelyn thought. 'Stop teasing! Pour the tea. It's your side, not mine.'

'Yes, I was afraid your hands would be too shaky to do it properly.' Simon sat up to carry out her order, but he had as usual had the last word, Jocelyn thought moodily. What a mass of inhibitions she was! Similarly placed, she felt sure Candida Melbourne wouldn't have cared a jot if the entire hotel staff had caught her kissing Simon.

Turning to hand over the cup and saucer, Simon saw

her rueful expression. As if he guessed what was in her mind he said consolingly, 'Never mind, Puss. Better to be modest than too much the other way. Some girls never learn man is by instinct the hunter.' For some reason, this pithy remark did more to make Jocelyn take heart than anything else Simon might have said. He could never accuse her of mooning after him, casting him melting looks as some of the students did or giving him what he termed 'the green light', and apparently this pleased him.

They breakfasted at their leisure and had a stroll before getting into the car to continue their journey. 'Highways or byways?' Simon asked as he started the engine, and at Jocelyn's impulsive, 'Well, we aren't expected until late afternoon,' he replied, 'Byroads it is, then. I agree, it's far too nice a day to miss all this lovely country, though we'll get plenty of that at Llantarwyn. Not stayed with the Pendletons before, have you?'

Jocelyn shook her head as she got out the map. 'You'll like them,' Simon continued as they drove out of the village. 'Pablo's father rarely goes out, but there's not much he doesn't know about world affairs,' then in answer to Jocelyn's questioning look. 'He's had polio. Didn't you know?'

'I don't recall Angie mentioning it to me.'

'Probably because after a few minutes in Julius Pendleton's company one tends to forget his infirmity. I'm surprised Angie didn't tell you, however, that it was as a result of saving her father-in-law from an accident when the brakes on his wheelchair failed that she stayed in Wales and fell in love. Pablo was a confirmed bachelor, but we all have to go in the end,' and Simon slanted a teasing glance sideways. Before she could think up an answer he went on, 'Come on, navigator. Which way?'

'Can we go via Ludlow? I've always wanted to look over the castle.'

'Your wish is my command.' The grey eyes were frankly provoking, but Jocelyn, refusing to rise to the bait, said simply, 'In that case we take the left turn at the next roundabout. We can cut across the M5 about ten miles further on and then it's secondary roads all the way.'

It turned out to be one of the happiest days Jocelyn could remember, for Simon's relaxed mood communicated itself to her and by the time Ludlow was reached she was chattering away as if she had never stood in awe of him for most of her adult life. Had he deliberately calmed her fear or was it something in the very air? Whatever the reason the barriers between them had vanished, if only temporarily.

During a tour of the ruins of what once had been one of England's strongest fortifications Jocelyn found herself talking without restraint while Simon encouraged her to state her views, argue with him, even contradict him without more than a whimsical lift of one dark eyebrow and a smile which Jocelyn could only describe as one of satisfaction lifting the corners of his mouth whenever he glanced at her expressive face. When they stood in the sunshine at the centre of what once had been the castle chapel, Jocelyn said, 'Did you know this is where Prince Arthur and Katherine of Aragon stopped when they made their wedding tour and where poor little Edward V was living when his father died and he was taken to London to be crowned? I wonder what really happened to the princes in the Tower. History relates that Edward was never strong. Perhaps he just died; they both could – natural deaths, I mean. No National Health in those days. And look at Prince Arthur. He died the year after he stayed here. Would he have made a better king than Henry VIII, do you suppose? It's strange, isn't it, to look around and imagine them coming in here for mass, playing ball on the green out there, hunting down by the river.'

She stopped with dreams still in her eyes and Simon chuckled. Jocelyn looked up as he tickled her cheek with a gentle finger. 'What a romantic you are! Your head's stuffed full of fairy tales. Life was probably a good deal harder than it is today, certainly for the poorer people. And as you say, no Health Service, even for the rich and mighty. And no plumbing.'

Simon shuddered dramatically. 'Has it ever occurred to you, my Queen of the Fairies, what life must have been like with no running water, no dry-cleaners or modern detergents? No wonder people carried pomanders round their necks and judges sat with bouquets of herbs when dispensing justice in case they caught the plague. While you're dreaming of Henry VIII and Anne Boleyn tripping the light fantastic, remember everyone, king and commoner, usually had at least three kinds of body lice in those days.'

Jocelyn's eyes widened in horror. 'Simon! You can't mean it?'

Simon leaned forward and softly kissed her parted lips. 'Sorry to chase away your illusions. Come on, forget your poor ghosts. After all, they'll never know what they missed,' and he held her hand as if by way of consolation as he led the way back to the car.

They stopped briefly for tea when well over the Welsh border, and five-thirty found them drawing up to the Pendletons' front door, where they were immediately engulfed in the warm family atmosphere. As well as Pablo's father, brother and stepmother, Angie's old boss Basil Beavis and his wife had arrived to attend the christening. Everyone had gathered in a sunny room at the rear of the house overlooking the extensive garden, and after all the introductions, Jocelyn found herself sitting alongside Bron Pendleton being studied by two bright, kindly brown eyes.

It was impossible not to feel at home under that friendly gaze and soon they were chatting like old acquaintances. It came as something of a surprise to discover that Pablo's stepmother had never even heard of Wadebridge's. Overhearing, Pablo came to lean over the back of the small settee they were occupying and say quizzically, 'Bron thinks the fashion scene frivolous, Jocelyn. She only tolerates my interest in it because I do occasionally do commissions of a more serious nature.'

'Of course it's frivolous,' Bron said indignantly, though her eyes smiled as they met Pablo's. She turned to Jocelyn again. 'How can girls waste their time acting as clothes-horses, their faces caked with goodness knows how many layers of cream and powder? You'd think they'd want to do something more worthwhile.'

'But it's all some of them are fit for, Bron *bach*,' Pablo teased. 'There are girls, alas, with no other ambition than to wear the latest fashions and if possible see themselves one fine day on the cover of a magazine. Isn't that right?' he appealed to Jocelyn.

'I'm afraid so,' Jocelyn admitted as Bron shook her head in disbelief. 'They're not all as silly as Pablo makes out,' she went on in mitigation, 'and some are so beautiful it's a pleasure just to look at them.'

Bron still looked unconvinced and Pablo laughed as he straightened. 'Save your breath, Jocelyn. You'll never persuade her that we don't show innocent girls the road to ruin. Bron, bless her, would like to see every girl under twenty-five with a diploma of nursing or some other similar certificate of true vocation.'

'Don't you believe a word he says,' Bron pretended to slap the hand lying on the back of the settee. 'Come along, my dear,' she said as she got to her feet. 'I'm sure you'd like to see your room before supper. We usually sit down about seven o'clock.'

Her departure seemed to be the signal for a general move by everyone in the room. Angie, after a startled glance at the clock, said, 'Goodness, is that the time?

Philip will be starving!' and made for the door, at which Pablo chuckled.

'I'll bet she finds our son still out for the count,' he remarked as he followed Jocelyn and his stepmother. 'He's done nothing but guzzle and sleep like a log since we arrived. It must be the good Welsh air.'

'Philip's certainly a very amenable baby,' Bron admitted as they climbed the stairs. 'Shall we just have a peep at him before I show you where I've put you and Simon?' and without waiting for Jocelyn's assent she tapped on a door at the head of the stairs.

Pablo was only too right. The baby, his eyes still tightly closed, was lying on the bed quietly submitting to having his nappy changed. The button nose, rosy cheeks and fluff of black hair on the small head gave Jocelyn a pang in the region of her heart. She had never given serious thought to what it would feel like to have a child of her own, and a glance at Angie's doting expression brought home the fact that she might not experience the pleasure of holding a son or daughter in her arms.

It was a subject she and Simon had never discussed. For all she knew he might expect the agency to be her baby, as it was his. She forced a smile. 'He's adorable, Angie, and I'm sure he's grown since I saw him last.'

Bron took her arm. 'For heaven's sake don't start Angie off! After supper she shall tell you how much weight he's put on and how he's already out of his first vests. If I'm any judge he's decided he's not going to put up with this indignity any longer,' and as if to prove her correct, Philip opened his mouth and let out a yell of disgust at being manhandled into clean clothes. Amid a burst of laughter Bron and Jocelyn left Angie to pacify her son in the only way he yet understood.

Bron led Jocelyn to a bedroom at the end of the landing, saying as she did so, 'The bathroom's next door. If I were you I'd stake a claim before the men come up. Let me know if there's anything you need. I must go and see how the meal is getting on,' and she was gone before Jocelyn was halfway through a sentence of thanks.

She was unlocking the cases when the door opened and Simon entered. His eyes twinkled when they alighted on the high brass bedstead. 'It seems to be our week-end for togetherness, wouldn't you say? It must be the "in" thing this year. Perhaps we ought to throw out those single beds at home.'

There was no answer to this, nor did Simon appear to require one. He walked over to look out of the window. 'It's lovely here, but I'd go mad with perpetual peace and quiet. Give me the big city every time.'

He sounded thoughtful as Jocelyn joined him to glance first at the view outside then back at his face. 'It takes all kinds to make a world and there's something to be said for both environments. Would you be as happy in London if you didn't know all this was waiting somewhere?' and she waved her hand towards the quiet fields, the rolling hills in the distance.

Simon continued to look through the window for a few minutes before he answered. 'Quite the little psychologist, aren't we?' The words were taunting. 'With men it usually depends on the location of the loved one. A shack in the country, an attic in the city, both are paradise if the woman of his choice is there too.'

Jocelyn turned away, unwilling to let him see how the words hurt. Candida, of course. Candida was in the city, so Simon couldn't stand the country, though Candida's room in the luxury hotel she patronized during her stays in London could hardly be described as an attic. 'Supper's at seven,' Jocelyn said at last when she had controlled her trembling lips. 'We'd better get a move on. The bathroom's free, I understand.'

She dressed carefully, using less make-up than usual since Bron Pendleton obviously disliked too much artificiality. It seemed her effort had not gone unnoticed, for when they joined the rest of the party in the sitting-

141

room for pre-dinner drinks, Angie said admiringly, 'I do like your dress, Jo. Where did you get it?'

The garment in question was in a soft apricot chiffon and had been bought just before her wedding. Jocelyn wrinkled her nose and said in an undertone, 'Where I get all my things – from a friend of Simon's mother. Sometimes I feel like running amok, but I guess I've got accustomed to doing as I'm told.'

'Well, wherever you get them, your clothes always look smart, and that particular colour certainly suits you. You must let me have the address, though where Pablo and I'll be during the next few months jeans will be more useful.'

'What do you mean?' Jocelyn asked, surprise in her voice.

'Pablo's going to break the news over dinner, so beware. Now junior is safely here, he's shutting the studio and we're going to take off for a world trip, catch on camera all those out-of-the-way beauty spots no one's ever filmed so far. Then when we come back all the alterations at the flat will be finished and he can settle down and write a book.'

'How will you manage with a tiny baby? Won't it be risky?'

'The doctors say not, but convincing Bron is going to take some doing. She brought the boys up, so she looks on Pablo and Gordon as her own sons.'

In the agreeable conversation round the dinner table Jocelyn had almost forgotten Angie's startling disclosure until they were sampling portions of Bron's featherlight pastry and Pablo looked across the table to announce quietly, 'This will be the last time Angie and I will be able to join in a real family party for some time, so I'm glad everyone was able to get down for the christening.'

Julius Pendleton looked up, his eyes keen, as Bron asked quickly, 'What do you mean?'

Pablo turned to his stepmother and smiled. 'You

always deplored my way of earning a living. I've taken your advice and when you hear our plans I'm sure you'll agree that what we propose doing is more worth while. I'm closing the studio for a year while Angie, Philip and I do a world trip. We'll be away twelve months, maybe longer.'

Bron's face was a study. 'But you can't be meaning to drag a . . .' She got no further as with a quick frown in her direction Pablo's father said, 'A splendid idea. If I weren't stuck in this confounded wheelchair, Bron and I would up sticks and come with you. Where are you thinking of making for?'

'Mexico for a start.' Pablo could not keep the gleam of enthusiasm out of his brown eyes. 'After that we'll play it off the cuff. Go where the spirit moves us and get everything of interest on film, of course,' he ended, looking slightly less imperturbable than usual.

Simon looked across at Jocelyn and she sensed a challenge in his voice as he announced, 'Jocelyn and I have not had a proper honeymoon yet. What do you say we take off when things have quietened down and join Angie and Pablo in Mexico?'

Jocelyn's noncommittal reply was lost in the shout of laughter and protest from Pablo and Angie as they declaimed all intention of playing gooseberry with a honeymoon couple, and when the laughter died down, to her relief Jocelyn found the subject had been dropped, she was sure at the instigation of Pablo's father. That Bron had been badly disturbed by the news had obviously not escaped him.

After coffee and liqueurs, Pablo suggested a walk, but Angie, cosy in the corner of the big four-seater settee, looked up with a laugh to protest, 'You and your walks! Philip will be ready for his feed soon, so count me out.'

Of the others, only Simon got to his feet and held down a peremptory hand to Jocelyn. 'Come along, darling, let's take a walk with Pablo. A breath of air will do us both good.'

How loving he sounded, Jocelyn thought with an inward sigh as with her hand in Simon's she went into the garden. Involuntarily they all stopped at the edge of the flagged portion outside the french doors. A huge full moon like a Hollywood film set illuminated the silent garden turning flowers and shrubs to silvery ghosts, while the little stream which ran at the bottom of the long sloping garden could be distinctly heard in the stillness. Only the flap of an owl's wings as it flew from one tall tree to the next broke the almost eerie silence.

'Wish I could paint it, just like this.' Pablo's sigh at his lack of artistic ability brought Jocelyn's head round to search his face. In the moonlight the Spanish blood inherited from his dead mother made him look more swarthy than usual. He suddenly turned his head to smile at Jocelyn as if regretting giving her a glimpse of his innermost frustrations and said lightly, 'I think I'll go and give Angie a hand after all. There's no need for you to miss the moonlight,' he added as he turned to re-enter the house.

Jocelyn felt her fingers growing numb. She tugged and Simon released her hand to put an arm round her waist and walked her briskly down the path. Propelled would have been nearer the word, for Jocelyn was out of breath by the time they reached the garden bench set under the trees on the bank of the stream and Simon pushed her none too gently on to it.

'For a moment there I thought you were contemplating going back into the house with Pablo. And you didn't exactly back me up when I suggested we honeymoon in Mexico. Couldn't you have managed to summon up a fond "that would be lovely, darling"?' or even a moderately affectionate smile of agreement would have done.'

Jocelyn sensed that the indulgent companion of the

afternoon had vanished as if he had never existed. Why was Simon suddenly behaving as if he were two men, Dr. Jekyll one moment, Mr. Hyde the next? Mr. Hyde certainly was uppermost as he lounged beside her on the bench to drawl, a note of almost insolent flattery in his voice as he said lazily, 'Angie was right – that dress certainly does do something for you,' and leaned forward to pull her towards him casually, kissing the soft skin where her neck and shoulder met.

She tensed automatically, knowing full well the response her uncontrollable body would make if Simon continued to make love to her. When his lips moved to cover her face with kisses she felt herself melt like wax, her whole body on fire, and it was only with the greatest difficulty she prevented tears of despair from overflowing.

There was no tenderness in Simon's lovemaking and the lips on hers were hard and demanding, so that at last she leaned against him, all resistance gone. He was obviously bent on teaching her a lesson, for he did not raise his head until Jocelyn, her mouth bruised by his ruthless kisses, made a small sound of protest. 'If anyone can see from the house,' he said cruelly, 'that ought to set any doubts at rest. Thank you, my dear, for a most enjoyable interlude.'

Jocelyn never knew afterwards why she did it, what gave her the sudden courage, but the unmerited insult made her act on impulse. The words were hardly out when the crack as her palm met Simon's face echoed round the arbour and she stared aghast at him, waiting for retribution to catch up with her.

But looking into his face, she saw his expression had changed. Instead of the anger she had feared there was no sign that he resented her reaction to his gibe. Dr. Jekyll was back. He leaned forward to straighten her dress, do up a button which had come unfastened during the struggle, and even flicked her hair into place before he stood to draw her to her feet. 'Sorry, that was uncalled-for. I promise not to misbehave again.'

When they walked back to the house it seemed to Jocelyn as if the gulf between them had widened, and not all of it was Simon's fault, she admitted to herself. As she got through good nights to the rest of the household and went up to bed the tears she had held back in the garden began to fall and she locked herself in the bathroom until she had her emotions under control, wishing she knew the secret of how to handle her unpredictable husband.

By the time Simon came up to bed Jocelyn had put into practice all the valuable lessons she had learned about skin care and her face and eyes showed no sign of redness caused by her bout of weeping. She was surprised to see the slightly apprehensive look Simon shot in her direction as she brushed her hair before the dressing-mirror. He might pretend indifference to her moods, but apparently he was not so unconcerned as he appeared.

He got undressed and slid into the big double bed without a word, however, and Jocelyn's spirits sank still lower. Subconsciously she knew in her innermost heart had been the hope that away from their usual preoccupation with the business, in the bosom of this happy family and with Candida's sparkling personality far away, Simon and she might have reached a better understanding. Instead everything she said and did only seemed to make bad worse, eat away at what little harmony existed between them.

The good fairies must have been on holiday when she was christened, Jocelyn thought as she turned out the overhead light. At that moment she would have given her right arm for just one of the virtues bestowed on more fortunate girls. That Simon might be regretting tying himself to such an also-ran crossed her mind as she slid out of her dressing-gown and climbed into bed beside him. But yet again, this enigmatical man surprised her by smiling, reaching out his arms and pulling her close. As he switched off the bedside light he whispered, 'Go to sleep, Godmother. There's a big day tomorrow.' Mr. Hyde really had gone, Jocelyn thought thankfully as she snuggled down and closing her eyes fell into a dreamless sleep.

CHAPTER SIX

IT was a big day, as Simon had predicted, and a busy one. The ceremony was to take place in the village church at three and all morning Jocelyn and Babs Beavis stayed in the kitchen to help Bron prepare buffet dishes for the friends and relatives who would be coming back to drink the baby's health. Lunch was a scratch meal with everyone anxiously searching for a sign of blue skies. To Angie's near despair the spell of fine weather seemed to have broken, for they had awakened that morning to the sound of rain on the window panes.

But as the luncheon dishes were being washed the first glimmers of sunshine appeared and by the time everyone was assembled for the journey to the church, garden and roads were drying rapidly. Jocelyn, wearing an emerald green dress, black court shoes and handbag and a wide-brimmed hat in green straw with chiffon roses round the crown, had no idea how pleasant a picture she made as Angie handed her the sleeping child. Eyes fast shut, wearing a be-laced family christening robe, Philip Pendleton looked like a small sleeping angel, and at Pablo's sudden 'Hold it!' Jocelyn looked up and smiled self-consciously as the shutter clicked.

'I hope it's only for the family album,' she confided under her breath as Simon helped her to slide carefully into the car, and a blush of pure pleasure rose to her face as he answered, 'Have a bit of faith in yourself for once, Puss. You look like the apple on the top of the tree in that outfit. Philip, when he's old enough to realize it, will be proud of his godmother. I already am.'

This unexpected compliment kept Jocelyn silent all the way to the church and during the service she was aware of Simon's eyes watching her thoughtfully. It was a good thing, she thought as she handed the baby to the rector, that Philip had not waked, for her attention was distracted from the job in hand by the look on Simon's face every time she happened to glance in his direction. He had hardly taken his eyes off her since they had entered the church and the steely regard unnerved her.

The ceremony over, Pablo took a whole reel of film while his brother's ciné-camera was levelled on family and friends alike until Simon interfered with a 'Let me take you for a change!' Back at the house it was by this time warm enough for most of the guests to wander out into the garden, and as champagne corks popped, Jocelyn relinquished her godson to Angie and accepted the glass Simon handed to her.

'Quite an exceptional baby, wouldn't you say?' Simon remarked. 'I seem to remember Susan's brats bawled all the way through their christenings, and everyone was more than ready for the bubbly by the time we got them home,' and he raised his glass as he spoke. 'Incidentally, Bron suggests we stay on tonight and make an early start in the morning. What do you say to getting up and off at six or thereabouts and having breakfast on the road? I can let Neville know we may be half an hour or so later than usual.'

Jocelyn looked down to hide the joy she knew was glowing in her eyes. No sense in letting Simon into her secret delight that the week-end hadn't been such a disaster as she had feared. She knew him well enough to guess that he would never have considered extending their stay had he been bored, and as he said softly, 'I take it that silence means consent?' she nodded, glad she had not yet taken off her hat and that the wide brim hid her expression. It would never do for Simon to catch her wearing her heart on her sleeve.

Guests living within driving distance began to leave by ones and twos as the afternoon wore on, and at six Jocelyn went with Angie to help get the baby out of his elaborate christening outfit and ready for bed. As she folded away tiny garments while Angie satisfied her son's healthy appetite, Jocelyn felt a thrill of pure envy. The room was quiet apart from the infant's greedy sucking and, unable to bear the sight of the absorbed maternal expression on her friend's face any longer, Jocelyn, with a 'Call me if you want anything. I'll only be next door,' went to her own room.

She sank down on the dressing-stool and studied her features in the mirror. Don't you know envy is one of the seven deadly sins, she told herself, so why the recriminations? You made your own bed, so stop looking sorry for yourself. Having a baby of your own would only complicate things still more.

She was darkening her eyebrows and lashes when Simon strolled into the room. 'Baby-worshipping over for the day?' he asked caustically. 'Thank goodness for that! I couldn't have stood much more. How you women drool over a new baby! They all look the same to me, like grapefruits with currants for eyes.'

Jocelyn was stung into a retort. 'How disgustingly indifferent you are to other people's likes and dislikes! What gives you the right to sit there like Jove on Olympus judging us mere mortals with such intolerance?'

But Simon was unperturbed by her outburst. He lay on the bed, hands beneath his head, and said, amusement in his deep voice, 'You look very pretty when you're angry. Did you know?'

Jocelyn, the mascara brush in her hand, swung back to face the mirror, sheer rage keeping her silent. What use to take Simon to task? He would go his own sweet way regardless of anyone's feelings except his own.

He surprised her, however, by asking, 'You're not really angry, are you, Puss?' He got up, strolled over and turned her to face him, studying her expression intently. 'Why, I believe you are. I didn't mean to catch you on the

150

raw. As babies go, Philip is quite an acceptable infant.'

'I'm sure Angie and Pablo would be most honoured to hear you say so,' her lip curled as she tried to draw away. 'However, there's no need to spare me your true opinion.'

The smile faded from Simon's eyes, but he still held her firmly turned to face him. 'I really seem to have inadvertently hit a nerve. Sorry – but you must know what I'm like by this time? You'll have to take me as I am, bear with my shortcomings.'

The anger faded from Jocelyn's eyes and she seemed to shrink within his hold as he bent and kissed her forehead before turning away. 'I won't spoil the fresh make-up. Finish your face. I really only came to tell you Bron has supper on the table, though why we need feeding again I don't know. We seem to have been eating all afternoon.' If Jocelyn hadn't known better, she'd have sworn there was a dejected note in the smoothe even tones.

As soon as supper was over, Basil and Babs Beavis said goodbye, and as Julius Pendleton expressed a desire for a game of bridge, Simon, Gordon Pendleton and Bron joined him round the baize-covered card table. Angie whispered in Jocelyn's ear, 'They'll enjoy it more if we're not chattering. Let's go and sit in Pablo's studio. We can talk as loudly as we like there and you can make us another coffee on that thingamajig of yours,' she continued, turning to her husband lounging on the settee beside her.

'No respecter of persons, my wife,' Pablo commented, but he got willingly to his feet and quietly shepherded the two girls through the garden door to the barn which was kept fitted out for his exclusive use. After an inspection of the photographs and pictures lining the walls, they drank black coffee and talked about the forthcoming trip, returning to the house some time later to find the bridge game abandoned.

'Who won?' Angie asked, going over to stand beside

her father-in-law, and Julius looked up affectionately to say, 'Simon and I routed them. Bron and Gordon hadn't a chance.'

'Not difficult to lose when you've Bron for a partner,' Pablo remarked, 'her mind's usually on tomorrow's menus or an Oxfam coffee morning,' and as his step-mother gave him a good-natured slap as he passed her chair he added, 'Never mind, love. There's more to life than playing a good hand of bridge,' to which his father added a heartfelt, 'Hear! Hear! How about something to drink before we all turn in?'

Jocelyn opened her eyes next morning to a kiss on the ear and a whispered, 'Time we were getting up.' She and Simon had said their goodbyes the night before, but when at last they crept quietly through the sleeping house Bron, a picnic basket in her hand, met them by the front door.

'I always get Julius a cup of tea at six. I thought it might be nice to stop for breakfast in a country lane rather than at a roadside café. You can let Pablo and Angie have the basket back and they'll return it next time they're down. Have a good journey,' and pulling her dressing-gown cord a little tighter she swung the oak door silently open on its well oiled hinges.

As they turned on to the road Simon asked, 'Enjoyed your week-end? It was nice of Bron to make us up a picnic breakfast, wasn't it?' and seemed to regard Jocelyn's simple 'yes' as an answer to both his questions, because as they reached the main road he settled in his seat and gave his undivided attention to the job of getting them back to London as quickly as possible.

Had she enjoyed the week-end? Jocelyn asked herself as the silence grew and the miles sped by. It had been a time of mixed feelings, at one moment imagining Simon's offhand compliments sincere, and at others hurt and lacerated by his deliberately cruel remarks. Perhaps she rose to the bait too readily. Certainly some if not all his comments might be construed in more ways than one. The trouble was she was too thin-skinned; had always been easily wounded by sarcasm or destructive criticism.

At least he'd not mentioned Candida and as far as she knew, not been in touch with her. If they were having an affair, Simon was being very discreet about it. Perhaps she should be thankful for that, thankful that he cared enough not to be blatantly open about the liaison. She suddenly became aware that Simon must have asked a question, for he was looking at her quizzically. 'You were miles away – when do you want to stop for breakfast?'

Jocelyn shook herself out of her self-absorption and smiled. She hoped Simon had not been able to read from her expression the thoughts which had been crossing and recrossing her mind. 'I leave it to you. Pull up when you want. I'm not particularly hungry, though coffee sounds attractive. I've suddenly realized I'm as dry as a bone.' The next crossroads led into a tree-lined side road and Simon swung the car left and pulled up in the space beside a field gate. Waist-high wheat waved in the early morning breeze like wind on water and as Simon reached into the back for the basket he asked, 'This do?'

Jocelyn turned to help inspect the contents of the picnic basket and replied, 'It may not appeal to a staunch supporter of the urban jungle, but I'll settle for it. Coffee?' and she unscrewed the top from the thermos flask.

As the mouth-watering aroma of freshly made coffee reached her nostrils, Simon handed her a mug and remarked thoughtfully, 'Talking of urban jungle reminds me. Those twins you interviewed last Thursday – did you enrol them?'

Jocelyn flashed him a look of complete surprise, her hand on the thermos suspended in mid-air. 'Yes, they start today. But how did you know?'

Simon smiled, mockery in his glance. 'I've not been

153

checking up on you, so don't get on the defensive! I merely happened to see them in Reception. You're going to have trouble with those two unless you keep them apart.'

'But they're such nice girls. Pretty too. I can just imagine them being a rave on T.V. commercials. They're so alike you can hardly tell one from another.'

'Exactly so,' Simon's tones were grimly ironical, 'and it's evident they detest it. How would you like to have a carbon copy of yourself always being beside you, having to share everything from leg-pulling to treats? Oh, it's fun, I daresay, to tease one's schoolteachers and friends, but that aspect of the relationship soon wears off. Take my advice, keep those two apart, put them in different classes if you can and get Carl to give them completely different hair-styles and Della a quite separate beauty chart.'

'But you know we try and fit cosmetics and hair to skin tones and types. The twins are so alike one of them is bound to look ridiculous with all the wrong cosmetics for her natural colouring.'

'Please yourself.' Simon sounded suddenly bored. He bit into an apple and turned to put the basket back on the rear seat. 'Just don't come to me to sort things out when they're at each other's throats, that's all.'

He started the car and drove in silence for the next hour, while Jocelyn sat miserably aware that she had once again fallen short of Simon's high standards. His mother would not have needed telling that the twins were jealous of one another nor required advice about how to handle them. Jocelyn remembered now that during the interview they had not been at their ease. Eager, yes, intelligent and suitable in other ways to become students at Wadebridge's, but they had not once looked at one another during the entire visit for enrolment, she recalled with dismay. No wonder Simon got impatient if he could recognize the storm signals in one short encounter. She, after a lengthy interview, had merely summed them up as two well-mannered girls looking for a career in modelling. Her knowledge that they could, if they wished, cash in on their remarkable likeness to one another had blinded her to a strained relationship Simon had instinctively detected.

It was a busy morning, but Jocelyn made time to go and have a talk with Della Cheriton about the controversial twins and since she had arranged with Carl to have a shampoo and set during her lunch hour, as he wound her hair on to rollers she asked his advice. He tied a net over his handiwork before he grinned into the mirror, meeting her eyes with mischief in his own. 'Don't worry, Jo. By the time I've finished, those two won't even recognize each other. Long brown hair, have they? Ever used a tint, do you suppose?' and as Jocelyn shook her head he lead her over to the dryer, whispering in her ear, 'This might be fun. Send them along this afternoon. I feel in the mood for experiments and you've given me an interesting challenge. As I'm always telling Della, hair is three-quarters of a woman's face. This will give me a chance to prove she's only got a quarter to play about with, for all her lotions and potions.'

Jocelyn hid a smile as the whirring of the dryer shut her away in a private world where no voices penetrated. She shut her eyes and dozed, wondering if Simon would be pleased by her submission to his recommendations in the car this morning. She would be openly magnanimous, she decided, and tell him she had taken his advice, but when she went along to his room later, the big office was empty.

Gwenda, returning from lunch, met her in the doorway. 'Did you want Simon? He went out right after he'd read his mail this morning. Candida Melbourne phoned just as he finished the most urgent letters. Neville's been dealing with his calls all morning. I thought you knew.'

'No, I've been busy myself. Give me a buzz when he

gets back,' and Jocelyn returned to her office to stare miserably out of the window.

So much for her high hopes! Candida had only to lift her little finger, it seemed, to bring Simon running, and on a busy Monday morning too – an unheard-of occurrence for a man dedicated to a set routine imposed as much on himself as on his employees.

Gwenda rang through about mid-afternoon to tell Jocelyn Simon had returned, but the impulse to confess she had taken his advice as regards the twins had long gone. 'I won't trouble him,' she explained as Gwenda told her Simon was between appointments. 'The problem's solved now anyway.'

At least that was the simple truth, Jocelyn thought as she replaced her receiver. Carl had sent the twins along for her inspection, and he had certainly performed a transformation in their appearance. Simon's recommendations were invariably sound, so why bother to tell him? Had she been hoping for a pat on the back? I'm getting like a puppy begging for scraps, she thought ruefully as Neville came into her office.

They spent the rest of the afternoon discussing arrangements for the first showing of a small collection of clothes for the under-thirties designed by two bright girls just out of art school. The object was to get at least one of the big chain store giants interested in this new range of dresses and blouses, but the girls' budget was limited, so the project needed some thought to cut expense to the bone without would-be buyers being given the impression of a 'shoestring' concern.

'Just one order from the John Bevis chain and they'd have more business than they could cope with,' Neville said. 'Which reminds me – Simon knows one of their managing directors, doesn't he? I'll get him to give him a ring. Nothing like the personal touch. Do you think you can arrange a write-up by one of the national dailies' fashion editors? That would be more your line than mine.'

Jocelyn was clearing her desk that evening when Simon walked in. 'Do you mind going on home without me?' he asked, then without waiting for her reply continued in a preoccupied way, 'I may be a little late. Don't wait for supper. I'll be home as soon as I can. Just push mine into the oven.'

Jocelyn forced a smile to joke feebly, 'Even if it's a salad?' wishing she dared ask where he was going. She was not reassured by discovering Neville as much in the dark as herself. 'Simon went off in rather a hurry. Aren't you going home together?' he asked as she was locking her filing cabinet.

'Not tonight.' Jocelyn's voice was flat and deliberately expressionless.

'In that case, how about a drink?'

Jocelyn managed a smile. 'Thanks, but not this evening. We were up at the crack of dawn. I intend having a hot bath and turning in early.'

Everybody had gone by the time Jocelyn had freshened her make-up. The usually humming offices and studios were silent and deserted, so the shrill ring of the telephone as she was crossing the reception area made her jump.

She walked over to lift the receiver and hear a voice ask for Simon. It was vaguely familiar. 'Sorry, I'm afraid he's gone.'

'And Neville Newton. Has he left too?'

Now Jocelyn recognized the voice. 'Is that Padwyn? Jocelyn here. Anything I can do?'

The answer was surprising. 'You don't happen to know the hotel Candida Melbourne's staying in, I suppose? You do! That's marvellous. Look, Jocelyn, Candida was pretty decent to me when I first came over here. Now I find I can return the favour. Will you ring her immediately and tell her I heard at lunch that Gloria's found out and is flying to London tomorrow? She'll know what I mean.'

Jocelyn was puzzled by the cryptic message, but it was really none of her business. 'Certainly I'll ring. Is that all you want me to say?'

'Yes, she'll understand all right,' even over the three thousand miles between them Jocelyn caught the 'no laughing matter' note in Padwyn's voice. 'There is one other thing. How's Neville?'

'Fine – why? Do you miss him?' There was teasing in Jocelyn's voice, but Padwyn's reply was lost as the line went dead. As she put the phone down to look up the number of the hotel, Jocelyn's face was thoughful. Had Padwyn really been cut off or had she hung up unwilling to answer the question?

It took several minutes to get put through to Candida's suite. The telephone rang for some time, to be abruptly answered by a man's uncompromisingly abrupt, 'Hello.' Jocelyn's hand moved almost without thought. One moment the receiver was at her ear, the next on its cradle – her automatic reaction to the sound of Simon's voice coming from Candida's room.

No sense in asking herself what he was doing there. But why brazenly answer the telephone? The answer was simple. He was indifferent to people's opinions and apparently similarly unconcerned about Candida's reputation. What did he possess instead of a heart? Jocelyn thought angrily as she almost tore the cover from Anne's typewriter.

Selecting a plain envelope and unheaded notepaper, she addressed a curt and brief message to Candida simply giving the information Padwyn had asked her to pass on. Twenty minutes later she was at the reception desk of the hotel, tipping a willing porter to take it up to her room.

Screened by a pot of ornamental greenery, Jocelyn awaited developments. Some ten minutes later, Simon and Candida emerged from the lift and walked across the foyer and out to a waiting taxi. Simon looked wooden and Candida, the huge fox collar of her cream evening coat turned up to hide most of her face, seemed bent on reaching the seclusion of the vehicle as soon as possible.

Jocelyn walked out to watch the conveyance disappear in the mass of traffic, then turned to make her own way home. At least there could be no doubt in her mind. Whatever was going on, Candida and Simon were in it together.

The telephone was ringing as she inserted her key in the door and as she picked it up, Janey's voice sounded in her ear. 'Are you alone, Jo? Thank heaven I've caught you at last!'

'Yes, Simon's out. What on earth's the matter?'

'Nothing alarming, but I've got Alan here. Can you come over? Oh, and Jo, bring some money.'

'Not again! What is it this time?' but the only answer Jocelyn received was Janet's urgent, 'If he's to catch the last train north tonight you'd better get your skates on.'

Jocelyn had replaced her 'rainy day' money in her handkerchief drawer and she grabbed it, stuffed it into her handbag and went out to get a taxi. It seemed like old times running up the stairs to the flat she had shared with Janey for so long, but her mind was preoccupied with Alan's latest exploit.

To her surprise, the door was opened, not by Janey, but by a strange young man who looked as if he had escaped from a rugby fifteen, and on going into the living-room, Jocelyn found another strange young man, even taller and heavier than the first, but who bore an unmistakable resemblance to the giant who had let her into Janey's flat. Alan was lying on the sofa with Janey bending over him. From the pleas of 'Don't!' and 'Stow it Janey, that hurt!' there wasn't much wrong with him, but when Jancy at last stood up and Jocelyn got a proper look at her brother, she let out a gasp of horror.

Janey had partially undressed him and Alan's upper half was covered with livid patches and adorned here and there with strips of sticking plaster. One eye was closing rapidly and Jocelyn did not doubt it would be a colourful purple by the morning.

'What have you been doing?' Jocelyn did not realize she sounded so schoolmistressy until one of the giants laughed and said in a deep pleasant voice, 'Like all sisters, isn't she, John?'

Janey, putting the top on a bottle of surgical spirit, interrupted, 'He got pushed down a flight of stairs at the inter-university athletic meeting and considering everything, he's come off remarkably lightly, so don't fuss, Jo. John and James were on the way to the coach too, but kindly stopped and picked up the bits. They didn't dare come to you in case Simon wouldn't be very sympathetic, so Alan got them to bring him here. Fortunately it's my day off, otherwise they'd have drawn a blank. Now the trouble is by this time their coach will have left and their tickets were on it. I've only got three pounds. If you can sub them for the time being, they can get back tonight by train.'

Silently Jocelyn opened her handbag and taking out all her loose notes, pushed them into the hand of the huge young man standing beside her. 'Thanks for rescuing Alan, and don't bother to return the money. I'm only too grateful to you and your brother for not leaving him behind. Was it a college outing?'

For his size he looked very boyish and pink-cheeked with embarrassment as he stuffed the notes into his pocket. 'Yes, that's why we had to ask your help. The bus was chartered by the college. We never expected to get landed with much expense, so we didn't bring much loose change. Now while James and I locate a taxi, can you get Alan back into his gear and downstairs? The last train won't wait and there isn't another until the milk train in the morning.'

Alan muttered confused apologies interspersed with exclamations of pain as Jane and Jocelyn between them buttoned him into his shirt, and pulled his jacket carefully over it. Janey giggled, 'I don't know what your tutor will say tomorrow! You look as if you've been in a free-for-all. I hope he'll believe your story.'

Alan pulled a face at her which obviously hurt, because he groaned as he stood up. 'Sure you'll be okay?' Jocelyn asked just as John put his head round the door and said, 'Taxi's at the door. Come on, Alan, let's be having you.'

'I should think after that you could do with a cup of coffee,' Janey remarked as the front door slammed. 'I know I could. Not worrying about Alan, are you, Jo? He'll be all right in a few days. I say, you *are* looking pale.'

Jocelyn laughed shakily. 'When you phoned I was just going to have supper. I only had a cup of coffee and a bun at lunch-time.'

'No wonder you look pale! You must be faint with hunger. Honestly, Jo, why can't you be sensible about meals? Where's Simon? I should have thought he'd enough sense to see you had at least one decent meal a day.'

'You mustn't blame Simon. We usually eat when he gets home. Tonight he had to go out, and I was late getting home.'

'I'll say!' Janey led the way to the kitchen. 'We tried to get hold of you several times before you answered. I even tried the office.' She looked down thoughtfully as Jocelyn pulled out a stool and sat down at the table. 'Come on, Jo, what's bothering you? You haven't the radiant bloom associated with most brides. Everything is going okay between you and Simon, isn't it?'

The sympathy in Janey's voice was Jocelyn's undoing. Tears filled her eyes and rolled down her pale cheeks. The omelette pan went down on the gas ring with a thump and the next minute Janey's arms were around her. 'Go on, have a good howl. It will do you the world of good. Sister says it's nature's finest safety valve.'

Jocelyn laughed amidst the tears, found a tissue and blew her nose. 'Sorry,' she apologized, 'but I've had one hell of a day and Alan was just the last straw.' She evaded the question about her relationship with Simon and added, 'Here, I thought you promised to feed me. Shall I do the omelettes?'

She got up as she spoke and Janey, after a shrewd glance at her face, replied, 'No, I'll do the cooking. Go and get us a drink. I think there's a bottle in the sideboard.'

When Jocelyn returned carrying two glasses of wine Janey had laid the table and a king-size omelette was sizzling in the pan. She divided it into two, put half in front of Jocelyn, slid into her own seat and picked up the glass. She sipped, grimaced and said, 'I told George that bottle was too cheap to be true. Still, it's better than nothing.'

'Where is the pride of the medical profession?' Jocelyn asked as she picked up her fork. 'I expected on your day off he'd be around.'

'Split duty,' Janey replied. 'He had to go on at four as someone went off sick. We'd got tickets for the theatre too. I gave them to one of the girls on the ward. She'd been trying to see the show for ages and couldn't get seats.'

'When he's free one evening, perhaps you'll bring him over to supper.' Even as she said the words, Jocelyn wondered whether it was wise to proffer invitations. She had no guarantee that Simon would even be there to receive guests; not if tonight's events were anything to go by.

When she arrived home, he was sitting in the big living-room and he watched in nerve-racking silence as Jocelyn walked across the room. He was evidently expecting an explanation of her absence and she stammered, 'I've been over to see Janey,' the mutinous feeling growing inside that while she was accountable for all her comings and goings Simon did not appear to think the arrangement should be mutual.

'Eaten, have you?' was all he said, and shook open the

newspaper. 'You look tired. Go to bed. I'll bring you a hot drink when you're in bed.'

Jocelyn walked on unsteady feet towards the bedroom. Would she ever fathom the workings of his mind? Women were supposed to be the contrary sex, but what could be more contradictory than Simon's usual attitude towards her, one minute the schoolmaster, the next offering to come and tuck her up like a kind uncle.

But there was nothing avuncular about his behaviour when he came in carrying a beaker of whisky and hot milk to sit on the bedside and study her with an unnervingly searching expression in his grey eyes. A corner of his mouth twitched, however, as he asked, 'Do you know you look about fifteen with your hair curly from the steam and in that prim night attire?'

Jocelyn ran a hand over her unruly locks, trying to make the wayward curls lie flat as she glanced down at the old cotton pyjamas which she had taken from the drawer in preference to the more glamorous trousseau nightwear which Simon's mother had chosen.

Now, looking up to meet the danger signals in Simon's eyes, she wished she had chosen something more seductive. She couldn't imagine Candida Melbourne in a home-made garment and it must be something of a letdown for Simon to return home to such a homespun creature as herself. In general Simon's mother had smartened up her outward appearance, but inside, Jocelyn often felt still the shy, naïve girl she had been five years ago.

What a contrast I must present, she thought as she picked up the beaker, then her eyes locked with Simon's again as she lifted the drink to her lips. 'What made you go to Janey's? I thought after our early start this morning and a day at the office you'd be ready to put your feet up.'

Here it came. The punch line behind the casual attentions. 'Janey rang. It was her day off and George was on duty.' No need to mention the real reason for her visit. Better by far to leave Alan's name right out of it.

'George? Oh yes! – her latest steady boy-friend.' Simon got up and began to take off his jacket. As he removed his tie he laughed unexpectedly.

'By the way, congratulations on taking my advice. You did a great job. I hardly knew them as they came out of the salon.'

Jocelyn wrinkled her brow and seeing her mystified expression Simon explained, 'The twins. You remember, I advised you to split up their identities.'

A relieved smile lighted Jocelyn's eyes. Back on safe ground she relaxed and answered lightly, 'Even I didn't realize how literally Carl would take me. When I saw one twin with blonde Afro curls and the other with sleek red hair I had to look twice to recognize them myself. Thanks for putting me wise.'

'Think nothing of it. Not every man is fortunate enough to have a sensible wife who accepts a bit of sound advice without argument. And has the courtesy to admit she was wrong.'

Sensible, Jocelyn thought, as she drained the beaker and relaxed against the pillows. Who wants to be thought sensible? When Simon returned from the bathroom she pretended to have fallen asleep and did not reply as he bent over her bed to whisper 'Good night.' He added a whispered word after the good night, but so softly she could not catch it. Had it been, 'Good night, love?' No, her hearing, muffled by the pillow, must surely have misled her.

The week flew by. Simon was inexplicably absent on several occasions, and Neville, coming in one evening to give her the latest news on the show for Lesley/Louise, asked, 'Has Simon said anything about contacting that friend of his at John Bevis & Co. to see the Lesley/Louise designs? Oh, and that reminds me. Lesley, who seems in charge of the administrative side of the business, thinks we might be able to hold the show in their own house. Apparently the firm's run from a place Louise inherited – designing, making, the lot. Lesley says the whole of the ground floor could be cleared if we think it a workable idea. Of course, it means going to see the place for ourselves and I wanted Simon in on it too, but Gwenda tells me he's out. Do you know where he's gone, or is he likely to be back?'

'Sorry, no idea.' Jocelyn doodled on her pad. Not for the world would she tell Neville she could probably find Simon easily enough. Wherever Candida was Simon would be too.

She was wrong, however, for at that moment the object of their thoughts strolled unexpectedly into the office. 'What are you two looking so serious about?' Simon asked, and Neville, after a quick glance at Jocelyn's impassive face, explained the proposed change of plan for the Lesley/Louise display.

'Arrange for the three of us to go over there, say around six tomorrow,' Simon suggested when he had heard him out. 'By the way, Bevis's are interested. I'm afraid I forgot to let you know.'

That for a start was most unlike Simon, Jocelyn mused as the door closed behind the two men. He was usually like a computer for detail and absentmindedness had never been amongst his faults. Candida must be proving so all-absorbing that she had put Simon out of his usually effortless stride.

As they were leaving the flat the next morning the postman arrived and Simon stuffed the letters into his briefcase saying, 'Come on. I must make a phone call at nine on the dot. We'll read these later.'

On arrival at the agency Jocelyn followed him into his office after picking up the office mail, and as Simon sat down to open his letters began to look at her own.

She was roused in the middle of reading an application from a star-struck schoolgirl of sixteen by a muttered expletive and looked up to be startled by a furious stare. Simon's eyes were almost black with rage as he flung the paper in his hand across the desk.

'So peeping and prying in the foyer of the hotel on Monday evening wasn't enough for you! Oh yes, I saw you hiding behind the hydrangeas,' his words bit. 'Apparently you had to hire a detective to see what I was up to when you couldn't spy on me yourself. More devious than you appear, like most females, aren't you? Well, I'm glad to see he's making you pay dearly for his services. I hope the information he supplied was worth it.'

Jocelyn looked down to see the receipt from Dick Walmer lying on the desk. Somehow it must have been addressed accidentally to Simon and not herself. This was no time to shield Alan. Judging by Simon's expression, their whole future was at stake. She opened her mouth to explain, but Simon's tired voice interrupted her before the first words of excuse could be uttered.

His eyes still smouldered from the violent anger which had surged through him as he said in an expressionless voice, 'Go away. I've no time to listen to the reasons for your petty jealousies. I'm sure you've plenty to do, so I suggest you go and get on with it.'

Jocelyn somehow picked up the receipt, her handbag and mail and controlling a pair of legs which threatened to give way walked through Gwenda's office and out into the rear corridor, her one idea to reach the sanctuary of her own office as quickly as possible. She let herself in and sinking into the big chair behind her desk she put her face into her hands and let the tears slide through her fingers.

How cruel and unkind could fate be? She had paid Dick Walmer's bill by cheque, not anticipating the arrival of a formal receipt. Drying her eyes, she picked it up. Simon could not have noticed the date of the account, but just the same, how quickly he had jumped to the conclusion that she was employing a detective to spy on Candida and himself. But was it so unreasonable a conclusion for him to reach, since it appeared he had spotted her in Candida's hotel watching for him only a few days earlier? Why had he not confronted her at the time? – but he had appeared to accept the explanation of a visit to Janey. Apparently he did not connect the message from Padwyn with her own presence in the hotel only a short time after its delivery.

Somehow Jocelyn got through the long trying day. There was no sign of Simon until, ready to leave to look over the Lesley/Louise premises, he joined Neville and herself with a terse, unsmiling, 'You two fit? Right, then let's get going.'

If Neville thought Simon's behaviour unusual he gave no sign, not even when they drew up at the old Victorian house in a rather unfashionable district and Simon asked half incredulously, 'Is this the place? They can't be serious about having a fashion show here.'

But his attitude changed after they were admitted, for while the exterior had little to recommend it, the interior was quite the opposite. Walls had been removed and borrowed lights included where possible, which with the addition of gleaming white paintwork gave an impression of space and an expanse in which to grow. An open-tread staircase led to the first floor where the now silent sewing machines were located. The girl who had opened the door was a redhead, small in every way, but what she lacked in inches was more than made up in a blithe self-confidence which Jocelyn could only secretly admire as she introduced first herself and then her partner Louise.

Lesley wasted no time in preliminaries, a point Jocelyn knew would be in her favour with Simon as she smiled up and said, 'Well, don't you think I'm right to think we can easily put our small show on here? Save not only the cost of hiring premises but all the trouble of taking the garments there. Three models should be sufficient. They can change upstairs and make their entrance down the staircase. As I told Neville,' Jocelyn noted that Lesley did not hesitate to dispense with the bother of surnames, 'we only want to land two really big orders for a start. I don't believe in running before you can walk. We can sell to some of the small boutiques, but it limits our reputation. An order from a big store with nationwide branches would get the Lesley/Louise label really well known and in addition cut costs in distribution. At the moment I take the things round myself in our van.'

There was an undoubted gleam of admiration in Simon's eyes and Neville was openly smiling with approval at this show of enterprise. Lesley might not be so inventive as her colleague, but she was obviously the drive behind the partnership, for Louise, quiet and dreamy, let her friend do all the talking. 'Come and see the workrooms. Louise and I sleep on the top floor and eat in the basement. We'll have a drink as soon as you've done the grand tour and get down to the nitty-gritty.'

Left alone, Jocelyn and Louise smiled at one another. 'Don't let Lesley put you off. We'd never have come this far without her. Oh yes – I do the designs, choose the materials, that sort of thing. But I've no head for business and thanks to her, we get along on a very small working capital. An old aunt left me this place. I was going to sell it, but Lesley got an architect chum to advise us and with friends' help you'd never believe how little it cost to renovate the place even at today's inflated prices. Come on downstairs and tell me what you think of our living quarters.'

She led the way to a door at the rear from where steps descended to what had once been a basement kitchen. Here too walls had been demolished and it was laid out as one vast living area with a sink and cooking facilities at one end. Yellow and white were the predominating colours and Jocelyn was admiring the unusual tiles and wall coverings when voices heralded the arrival of Lesley,

Simon and Neville.

As drinks were poured and Louise produced sandwiches and hot sausage rolls, Simon and Lesley between them discussed and arranged the final details for the showing of their designs. He somehow managed to ignore Jocelyn completely, though only she was aware that Simon had sent her to Coventry. He never addressed her once during the entire time they were in the house, and later, when Neville had dropped them off at the flat, the silence between them became almost a tangible thing.

For once, instead of the usual feeling of guilty self-condemnation Jocelyn began to feel angry. To be treated as a naughty schoolgirl when one has made a foolish mistake was one thing, to be taken to task without a hearing another, and as Simon helped himself to a drink she eyed his back with a fulminating glance as she asked icily, 'Would you like some cold meat and salad, or aren't you hungry? I asked Mrs. Telford to leave it ready, so it will only take a moment to get it on the table.' Her tone indicated that she hardly cared whether he ate or starved, and Simon swung round, a hint of surprise on his face, to look across the room with more than his usual penetrating stare.

Impassively Jocelyn remained motionless, then as he did not answer, turned towards the kitchen again. He followed to lean and watch in silence as she made a dressing, tossed lettuce and tomato in the big wooden bowl and then started to carve the cold chicken.

As if roused from some inner deliberation Simon immediately put down his glass, took the carving knife and fork with a terse, 'My job,' and began to slice the bird, Jocelyn relinquishing the carving without protest to carry the salad, bread, butter and cutlery out to the dining area. By the time Simon joined her, two plates loaded with slices of chicken in his hands, she had set the table.

'Rather a jolly little thing, wasn't she? Bright too. Louise is a clever designer, but too dreamy to get far on her own.'

In the midst of buttering a slice of bread Jocelyn paused to look across the table. 'Fancied Lesley, did you?' She was surprised at the tartness in her own voice.

Simon's head jerked up and he stayed immobile for twenty electric seconds as their eyes met. 'What's got into you, for heaven's sake? First you have me followed, now you're accusing me of taking a fancy to a girl I've met for one short half hour. It's not like you.'

'No, it's not.' Jocelyn almost threw her butter knife on to the table. 'I must be a disappointment, not turning out the mouse like little yes-girl you expected? You forgot one thing when you selected me as the girl most likely *not* to be an interfering wife. You forgot even worms have feelings.'

To Jocelyn's chagrin, Simon laughed. But his laughter contained no amusement and it grated on her already overwrought nerves. Just as she was wondering if she had gone that little bit too far the telephone shrilled, and throwing down his napkin, Simon got up to answer it. Jocelyn strained to overhear, but Simon's laconic replies gave her no indication as to the caller's identity.

He put the receiver down and turned. 'I'm afraid I've got to go out right away. I shouldn't be late, but don't wait up.'

'Go out? Now? In the middle of a meal?'

Jocelyn's indignation was plain to hear and Simon smiled mockingly. 'Yes. Sorry to have to halt you in mid-stream. You were doing very nicely in the role of a virago, but I'm afraid I can't stop for the epilogue.'

As his hand reached the doorknob Jocelyn's voice halted him. 'Simon, if you go out now without telling me where you're going or what it's all about, you'll leave me no alternative.'

There was no mistaking the threat in her voice and Simon's hand left the door handle as he walked slowly to stand looking down at her, his face grim. 'You have a bath, do your face – anything you like – but don't ask questions. And above all, don't do anything we'll both regret later.' The grim expression softened a little as he added, 'Try and trust me, Puss. Just this once,' and before Jocelyn could sort out her bewildered thoughts he had gone.

CHAPTER SEVEN

It seemed deafeningly silent in the flat after the front door slammed behind him, so that Jocelyn turned up the sound on the television as she cleared away the half eaten meal. Her appetite had faded with Simon's unexplained departure and though she tried to fill in time by washing up, looking out clean things for next day and sorting the laundry, when she looked at her watch only an hour had gone by. She was startled by the ring of the telephone as she was making herself coffee some half hour later and picked up the receiver with some trepidation.

To her surprise Janey's voice came over the line. 'I thought you'd be out with George, but from the sounds in the background you're on duty,' Jocelyn said after they had exchanged greetings.

'Yes, I got called to fill in at Casualty. There's a minor 'flu epidemic raging amongst the nursing staff. Look, love, don't be alarmed, but we admitted Simon a short while ago. Nothing to worry about, just a broken arm. They're taking him up to set it in theatre now, so I volunteered to give you a ring.'

'How on earth did it happen?' gasped Jocelyn.

'Accident! We're on take-in tonight, so they were all brought in here.'

'They?' Jocelyn's tone was a question and there was a pause before Janey replied.

'Yes. Quite a collection, in fact. Your Simon, Candida Melbourne, a Mr. Peter Dewsbury, one concussed ambulance driver and one very shaken drunk, all in one grand pile-up, apparently. Still, it stops us getting lazy.'

'Should I come, do you think?' Jocelyn asked, then half to herself, 'What was Peter Dewsbury doing, I wonder?

He's the firm's legal eagle – fixes all our contracts, things like that.'

'Is he?' Janey had overheard the quietly spoken words. 'Yes, I seem to remember you mentioning him. Bit concussed, though no bones broken. We're keeping him in overnight too, just in case. No, don't come. Simon will be too doped to know, so save it until the morning. And don't worry, it's not serious. See you,' and Janey had rung off.

Jocelyn put the telephone down slowly. So much for Simon's coaxing 'Trust me!' What a fool she was to fall in with his wishes if he so much as crooked his little finger. Well, this time he wasn't getting away with it. He would have to choose once and for all. No cake and ha'penny as well. Jocelyn was not aware that her face hardened as she decided that whatever the outcome of the affair with Candida, Simon would have to be taught a lesson. His little pushover of a wife had reached the end of her patience.

Her mind made up, Jocelyn went to bed, though her sleep was disturbed by distressing dreams, and the empty bed beside her when she woke brought back the events of the previous evening. An early call to Neville led to him picking her up for the drive to the hospital and when she arrived there the ward Sister was understanding enough to bend the rules and let Jocelyn in to see Simon out of the normal visiting hours.

As they entered the small side ward it was obvious that Simon had been teasing the young nurse busy remaking his bed, for a giggling rejoinder was abruptly broken off as the girl saw her superior in the open doorway. With a warning, 'Only a few minutes, I'm afraid, Mrs. Wadebridge. Rounds start in twenty minutes,' Simon and Jocelyn were left alone.

He looked much as usual, Jocelyn decided, apart from the arm in plaster and a bruise high up on his forehead. 'I didn't expect you this early.' His smile on any other occasion would have melted Jocelyn's susceptible heart. 'Come to soothe my fevered brow?'

'Hardly. Since I understand Candida is also an in-patient, I'm sure I can safely leave that in her capable hands.'

A gleam, it could have been anger or admiration, came and went in Simon's grey eyes, but so swiftly Jocelyn thought she could have imagined it.

'Peter Dewsbury's here too. Is she to soothe him as well?'

'Since she has two uninjured arms I wouldn't put it past her to try,' Jocelyn replied sweetly.

'In that case, to what do I owe this pleasure?' Now certainly the old sardonic note was apparent in Simon's voice.

'Merely for the look of the thing. As I'm a well disciplined wife wouldn't everyone have thought it odd if I hadn't turned up to see how you were? In any case, as you can't come to the office today Neville and I must be briefed.'

'Not necessary. I'm only here until the registrar's had a look at me and then Peter and I will be discharged. Sister tells me he's quite okay this morning and since I feel fine apart from the arm we'll both be allowed out.'

'Good, then I'll see you later. By the way,' Jocelyn turned in the doorway, 'why was Peter along?'

'Didn't your tame bloodhound report?' There was a grim note in Simon's voice which caught like a raw nerve. Controlling an impulse to slam the door to shut away the black temper on his face, Jocelyn retreated, hoping Neville would not remark on her hot cheeks and air of distraction.

He gave her a sharp glance as she slipped into the passenger seat beside him, but diplomatically made no comment, not even to her terse, 'Simon appears in good shape apart from his arm and will be back amongst us about mid-morning.' They drove to the agency in silence and to Jocelyn's mild surprise Neville followed her into her office and firmly shut the door. 'While you were seeing Simon I bought a morning paper. I don't believe you've seen this.'

He laid out one of the national dailies on the table as he spoke open at the middle page. The headline sprang up at her. 'Producer's wife KO's actress,' and beneath it a photograph of Candida alongside that of an unknown woman. Jocelyn picked up the paper and read the column beneath. It was short and to the point. 'Gloria Smith, wife of the television producer Arthur Aloysius Smith, was involved in a brawl last evening at a West End hotel when she knocked out up-and-coming television actress Candida Melbourne. Miss Melbourne, accompanied by two friends, was on the way to hospital when the ambulance was in collision with a private car. The occupants of the ambulance and the car driver were admitted to St. Ninian's Hospital, where Miss Melbourne's condition was stated to be satisfactory.'

There was bewilderment in Jocelyn's eyes as she raised them to find Neville watching her. 'What does it mean? Simon didn't explain. I thought ...' She stopped, unwilling to reveal exactly what she had imagined to be the true facts.

Neville took the paper out of Jocelyn's nerveless fingers and gazed at the printed page. 'Odd, but it looks like the old, old triangle. I knew there was trouble over Candida's contract with Arthur Aloysius, because I happened to overhear Simon discussing it with Peter Dewsbury the other afternoon. Simon and he must be the two friends referred to. Looks as if the fair Candida for once made a play for the wrong man. Gloria Smith appears to have a mean right hook, for an ambulance to be required.'

'I daresay the management of the hotel arranged it. They wouldn't care for that sort of publicity. Oh, Neville – I've suddenly remembered. Padwyn phoned from New York and asked me to give Candida a message about

Gloria Smith coming to England. Now I see why. What an ass I've been!'

'Aren't we all from time to time? Don't worry, it will all work out,' he smiled a reassuring smile as if he sensed the emotional tangle she was in.

But would it? Jocelyn was not so sure. Simon had it firmly in his head that she had been spying on him. That alone would be an unsurmountable obstacle to explanations at this late date. And how much did Candida's involvement with this Arthur Aloysius Smith touch him personally? Perhaps under the armour plating of his caustic exterior lay a heart as sore as her own.

But Simon nursing a sore heart was something at which her mind boggled. He was like the Jolly Miller in the old song, 'I care for nobody, no, not I, and nobody cares for me.' The last part at least was wrong, Jocelyn thought as she tried without much success to concentrate on the day's work. One person cared a great deal, and much good it did her.

Try as she would to grapple with the day's problems, Simon's face kept getting between her and her work. Suddenly, the twins' aversion to one another, the show for Lesley/Louise, the eager applicants who called to be interviewed seemed unimportant, and Jocelyn would have given a good deal to be able to get up and walk away from her responsibilities and the dilemma of the situation which had grown up between Simon and herself.

But common sense told her that to run away would solve nothing; she had to stay and see things out. The fact that she had misinterpreted his apparent obsessional interest in Candida was small comfort. All through the morning Jocelyn's mind kept wandering to what she was to say when Simon finally turned up, how she was to apologize. She concocted several imaginary speeches in her mind, only to discard them all when they finally came face to face.

176

Coming out of her office just before one, she was in time to see him disappearing into his office and she followed, closing the door behind her. Simon looked up as the door clicked to and Jocelyn's heart sank at his shuttered expression. Instead of the carefully prepared words of contrition she blurted out, 'Why didn't you tell me what was going on? I thought . . .' she stopped, because Simon had made a gesture of impatience as he sank into his swivel chair.

'You made it abundantly clear what you thought. If you must have it in words of three letters, I didn't want you involved in any way in the nasty business, but I suppose you've seen the report in the paper. Candida didn't realize all the finance for this T.V. series came from Gloria and that Arthur Aloysius can do nothing without her say-so. When things really began to get sticky I got Peter along as well to try and make Candida see sense. As you know from the press this morning, we both failed.'

It was a long speech for Simon, not as a rule given to explaining his actions, and it kept Jocelyn silent from sheer surprise. He smiled crookedly as if he too was amazed at his own loquacity. 'I'm afraid you wasted your money hiring that detective.'

'I didn't hire him to spy on you,' Jocelyn blurted out, and Simon frowned.

'Why, then?'

Jocelyn clenched her hands in misery. Now would come the condemnations at her stupidity. 'I hired him to find my engagement ring. While you were in the States I lost it.'

Her admission had the last result Jocelyn expected, for Simon began to laugh and, still laughing, got up to turn his back and stare out of the window. 'That will teach me to have less conceit!' He turned to face her again and it struck Jocelyn that he looked pale now the laughter had died. 'You'll laugh when you know what I imagined. Though I was furious that you'd set a detective on to me

I was presumptuous enough to assume that you were becoming interested in me personally at last, that your action was due to twinges of jealousy. Now I find all you were bothered about was retrieving a paltry ring. What I can't fathom is why you didn't just tell me at the time.'

The impenetrable barrier was between them again and as of old, it rendered Jocelyn tonguetied. Oh, to have had the courage to admit laughingly that she felt a good deal more than a mere twinge every time he looked at a pretty girl, or even just an attractive extrovert like Lesley of Lesley/Louise. But her dread of snubs from Simon still lingered, so that she merely said lamely, 'You don't look too well, Simon. Why don't you go home and rest? We can manage,' and was not surprised when this elicited the sort of reply she associated with Simon in one of his less amenable moods – an offhand, 'Spare me the solicitude. You know I can't bear being fussed over,' as he sat down again with an obvious air of dismissal.

The arctic atmosphere between them persisted for the remainder of the week and Jocelyn, in an endeavour to push her personal problems to the back of her mind, worked harder than ever, often staying on to finish jobs which could quite easily have waited. At work she was sure of Simon behaving with at least a veneer of civility, but once in the flat he withdrew again behind the invisible wall which had grown up between them.

One evening, Jocelyn's overwrought nerves could stand it no longer. It had been a more than usually difficult day at the office, as Fay had suddenly announced her intention of leaving and Della, normally one of the most imperturbable members of the staff, had had a difference of opinion with a troublesome student and Jocelyn had discovered her indulging in a bout of tears in a corner of the beauty shop. Calming Della down, reprimanding the student and persuading Fay to delay her departure at least until another receptionist could be trained had whittled Jocelyn's reserves to breaking point.

When they reached the flat that evening it was apparent that Mrs. Telford had not been in. The breakfast dishes still lay in the sink, and it was the last calamity of an impossible day when Simon delivered the *coup de grâce* by asking, 'How long until supper?'

Jocelyn, her face set, turned and spat like an angry cat. 'If you'd one shred of concern, you'd have suggested taking me out for dinner. But no,' her usually calm voice was harsh with sarcasm, 'I'm only sensible hardworking Jocelyn. No candlelit supper for her after a gruelling day slaving in your wretched agency. Well, I've taken as much as I can stand. As soon as I can get a place I'm moving out. Our marriage was a mistake right from the start. I should never have agreed to the bargain. It would have been better if I'd taken Alan's problem to Dad, however angry he might have been.'

Her voice faltered as Simon asked icily, 'Quite finished? Good. Then perhaps we could have something to eat. A poached egg will do.'

'Get it yourself!' Jocelyn said tearfully, and running into the bedroom she slammed the door. She sat on the side of the bed aghast at her own selfish lack of concern. Simon had probably been as tired as herself and had, she suddenly realized, looked unusually weary. Instead of helping she had turned her claws on him like the 'Puss' he teasingly called her. Determined to make her peace, she got up and hurried out just in time to see the door of the spare room close quietly.

Jocelyn stood and looked at the closed door through a mist of tears. Apparently she was not the only one who had taken as much as they could stand. This time she had lost Simon for good. He wasn't the sort of man to get down on his knees and plead.

The next two weeks were the most miserable Jocelyn could remember, and it was small consolation to know

179

that the course of action to which she was now committed was due to her own impulsive outburst. She had always been sorry for an inability to speak up for herself; when in the heat of anger she had plucked up sufficient nerve at least to speak her mind she could hardly have chosen a worse moment.

Simon was not the type to crawl to any woman, least of all to her, and it did not help to see the shadows under his eyes each morning as if he too had passed a sleepless night. If Jocelyn could have been sure his general air of malaise was on account of her imminent departure perhaps she might have had the courage to tell him that she didn't want to leave, but at the back of her mind lurked the suspicion still that he had gone to Candida's aid because he in his turn nursed a hopeless passion for someone who did not reciprocate his devotion. If this were the case, he had all Jocelyn's sympathy.

Wasn't that precisely her own position? She longed to put her arms around Simon, tell him she loved him, draw that dark head on to her breast and try and chase away his miseries. Instead, she felt obliged to behave with rigid self-discipline, desperately afraid that if Simon guessed he might find it cause for embarrassment or worst of all, amusement.

So reluctantly she scanned the newspapers to find somewhere to live, and was lucky enough to spot a bed-sitter to let near enough to the centre of London to obviate long journeys to and from work. As she looked over the tiny bathroom and kitchen which adjoined the bed-sitting-room at the top of an old Victorian house her feelings reached rock bottom. She had never lived alone, and the mere thought panicked her. As she sat on the bed, contemplating the comfortable but impersonal furnished room, it occurred to her that probably Simon expected her to look for alternative employment as well as an alternative home. It could cause endless embarrassment, Jocelyn suddenly realized, for him to have an estranged wife under his feet during the day.

But his manner made it impossible to bring up such a controversial subject. Apart from asking her if she still meant to go, he had not once mentioned her departure. He was polite, considerate and totally unreachable. Jocelyn missed his teasing, the maddening way he used to call her 'Puss' and 'Kitten'. Now he seldom called her even by name, and for this Jocelyn knew she had herself and only herself to blame.

The day before she was due to move out, she returned to the flat alone. Simon had dismissed her at the office with an abrupt, 'Tell Mrs. Telford to leave my meal in the oven. I may be late.'

So he wouldn't even share their last supper as man and wife, Jocelyn thought drearily as she pressed the button in the lift. What a fool she had been to force a showdown! Even living in misery with Simon was better than living without him. She put her key in the lock and immediately and instinctively sensed all was not as usual. For a start there was no sound from the kitchen. Normally Mrs. Telford's movements as she put the finishing touches to a meal were the first sounds to reach one's ears.

Then there was a fragrance. Jocelyn paused in the hallway and sniffed for the door leading to the living-room was open. There was no mistaking that perfume. Only one person used it, Simon's mother. Jocelyn walked slowly through the open doorway and found her sitting in a chair beside the big picture window.

'Don't look so surprised, my dear child. I arrived about an hour ago – Mrs. Telford let me in. By the way, I've sent her home. Forgive the interference, but I wanted to have a talk with you without an audience. Simon when I telephoned him two days ago gave me some information which made me think a third person was needed to straighten out a thing or two. Frank and I talked it over, so here I am.'

'It's not like Simon to go crying to Mummy.' Jocelyn's

tone was uncharacteristically sarcastic, but to her surprise, Simon's mother laughed, real amusement in her eyes.

'Yes, I agree, which just goes to show how desperate he's feeling. I don't recall him coming to me for help since he was fifteen, and he might not even have done so now had I not detected from his tone of voice that something was very wrong. Simon thinks he can deceive most people if he sets his mind to it, but his voice always gives him away to me. I wouldn't hang up until I had the whole thing out of him. When he said since you didn't love him he couldn't stand in your way, I knew I had to come. I think you do, and I don't think you realize, you silly child, that Simon took a shine to you when you were a teenager, though at the time he was so ashamed of his feelings that he wouldn't admit it, even to himself. When we decided to start up the agency, risk our savings, it wasn't for economy's sake that he picked a raw girl to be his first receptionist but because he was already half in love with you. And why all the obsession about you having the latest hair-styles, the lessons in make-up, the clothes he has provided over the years?'

Jocelyn dropped into a chair. 'But I thought that was your idea, and that the clothes were more or less a uniform, if you like, to make a good impression on clients and students alike.'

'If they were, why weren't Gwenda, Anne and Fay treated the same way? Of course something had to be done about the gypsy outfits you seemed to think suited your style. You used to look as if you were just off to join a hippy group. No, Simon imagined good clothes would give you confidence, help to chase away that chip on your shoulder that you weren't as attractive as other girls.'

Jocelyn smiled wryly. 'Well, let's face it, I'm not. And perhaps working where charm and beauty is the criteria didn't help. How can anyone like me compete with girls who have everything?'

'Ah, now we come to the crux of your problem, my dear. Since when has anyone had everything? Look around you. How many of our so-called beauties have brains? How far would any of them get without the backing of a good manager or agent? And the ones with brains – have they hearts? Very rarely. They seem to carry a stone, or perhaps I ought to say a computer, where their hearts ought to be, for they'll use anyone and everyone to get what they want, regardless of the hurt they may do. Simon said he'd done everything he knew to get you to stay, make you love him just a little, but that you mistrusted him too much. I'm not so sure myself, otherwise why did you stay at the agency? You could get a job anywhere. I'm right, aren't I? You don't hate my son?'

Jocelyn couldn't answer. Tears filled her eyes and she was afraid to speak in case they overflowed. Simon's mother smiled gently and held out her arms. 'Come here and tell me all about it.'

Jocelyn needed no urging. As she knelt beside her mother-in-law's chair out it all spilled – the misunderstandings, Candida's supposed influence, the final quarrel. 'Now he'll never forgive me. I said some pretty rotten things – but I wanted to hurt him. Stupid of me, wasn't it, because in hurting Simon I think I've just about broken my own heart. Ever since I've been walking around like a zombie wishing I'd the courage to chuck myself in the river.'

Simon's mother smiled down into the tear-filled eyes, her own looking very much like Simon's as she said, 'Don't do that. In any case, hearts don't break. But Simon will convince you of that much better than I ever could. Won't you?' she finished, looking over Jocelyn's head.

Giving a gasp, Jocelyn turned her head. Standing silently inside the room was Simon, and his face held an expression she had never seen before. In the midst of her weeping confession she had not heard his key in the door, How much had he overheard? She jumped to her feet, blowing her nose defiantly and saying disjointedly, 'I must look a mess. I'll do my face and see to supper.'

As she hurried for the door Simon put out his good arm and stopped her in mid-flight, jerking his head at his mother in a typically Simon-like gesture of dismissal. Getting to her feet, Betty Wadebridge Lexington smiled. 'I'll see to the supper. Take your time. It won't be ready for about half an hour.'

When she had gone, conscious of tear-stained cheeks and red-rimmed eyes, Jocelyn raised her chin and said, 'Wasn't it a surprise, having your mother drop in like this?'

'Yes, wasn't it?' Simon's tones were mocking. 'As surprising as hearing you felt like committing suicide. What an idiot you are!' Then as he felt her stiffen, 'What idiots we both are! Oh, what's the point of this stupid conversation? I only want to kiss you, my darling. Or hasn't it sunk into that obstinate head of yours yet that I love you? Have done since you were a gangling seventeen-year-old, God help me.'

'You've kept it very successfully to yourself, then – and why take so long to tell me?'

For answer Simon said, 'Shut up,' softly and gathered her to him, surfacing some three minutes later to say, 'Yes, why didn't I? Because, my sweet, I suppose I'm as obstinate as you. To start with I dreaded being accused of cradle-snatching, so I decided to give you time to grow up. When I thought you'd lost your childhood inhibitions I found you prickly, aloof and distrustful of me. You'd put up barriers round yourself that I couldn't break down. Alan's fall from grace was a godsend, gave me the excuse I'd been looking for to tie you down. I thought once we were married, I'd soon be able to change your attitude towards me, but in some ways you seemed more afraid of me than ever.'

'I was more afraid of giving myself away than of you, for it never occurred to me you were marrying me for any other reason than convenience. You needed someone to replace your mother, not only in the office but here, and who more suitable than readily to hand, useful, well drilled Jocelyn? Why didn't you give me just one little hint?'

Simon let her go and put a hand to his head as if this question was the last straw. 'Give you a hint? Give me strength! Have you any idea how difficult you are to convince? Both Walter Hook and Neville guessed how much in love with you I am. But what would you have done had I announced eternal devotion? Run like the devil or laughed in my face, I daresay. The longer I left it, the harder it became for you to regard me as other than the ogre in the inner office. You'll never have any idea how frustrating these last weeks have been. I thought a game of "Softly, softly catchee monkey" would break down your defences. I think now I should have stormed the fortress.'

He laughed and took her back into his one serviceable arm, looking down into her eyes with a gleam in his own which made Jocelyn's heart beat faster. His grey eyes seemed almost black as he asked, 'Convinced now, you tantalizing Puss?' to which of course there was only one answer.

They were brought back to earth by a laughing voice saying, 'Can you lovebirds drag yourselves back to earth long enough to come and eat supper? It won't keep a minute longer,' to which Simon prosaically answered, 'Mother, if this wayward contrary woman is anything like as hungry as me, we could eat a horse. I'm ravenous!' to which Jocelyn added, 'As I suspected. No heart, only a stomach,' as they joined Simon's mother at the table.

'I'm mad, of course, to give in so meekly.' Jocelyn went on, to which Simon replied with a snort of disgust.

'That's something you will never be again. Meek! You look capable at this moment of taking on all comers. Don't you agree, Mother? In a year I shall most probably be thoroughly hen-pecked.'

'Stop talking rubbish, the pair of you,' Simon's mother ordered, 'and eat. Or I shall be tempted to get the next plane home instead of staying to help Neville run the agency while you two have the proper honeymoon you should have had weeks ago.' She laid two travel vouchers on the table. 'Frank has a friend with a villa in Bermuda. It's yours for the next couple of weeks.'

She glanced bright-eyed from Jocelyn to Simon. 'What, no arguments? No excuses that you can't manage it at such short notice? Good! Now eat your supper like good children.'

Jocelyn turned her head to meet the laughter in Simon's eyes. In a suspiciously mock small boy voice he said, 'Wouldn't you say this is a case of "where Mother knows best"?' then he burst out laughing, leaned to kiss his mother's cheek and add softly, 'thank you. From both of us.' He took Jocelyn's hand in his and raised her fingers to his lips. 'I can see I should have solicited your help long ago,' he added audaciously, 'for it seems to me it takes a woman's intuition to get to the root of a problem.'

Simon's mother had the last word as she turned to Jocelyn. 'Never let him forget he said that and you're home and dry, my dear,' then raised her glass to toast the two sitting hand in hand on the other side of the table.

A GREAT IDEA!

We have chosen some of the works of Harlequin's
world-famous authors and reprinted them in the
3 in 1 Omnibus. Three great romances —
COMPLETE AND UNABRIDGED — by the same
author — in one deluxe paperback volume.

Essie Summers

Bride in Flight (#933)

. . . begins on the eve of Kirsty's wedding, when a
strange telephone call changes her life. Blindly,
instinctively, Kirsty runs—but even New Zealand isn't
far enough to avoid the complications that follow!

Postscript to Yesterday (#1119)

. . . Nicola was dirty, exasperated and a little bit
frightened. After her amateur mechanics on the car she
was in no shape to meet any man, let alone Forbes
Westerfield. He was the man who had told her not to
come.

Meet on My Gound (#1326)

. . . is the story of two people in love, separated by pride.
Alastair Campbell had money and position—Sarah
Macdonald was a girl with pride. But pride was little
comfort to her after she'd let Alastair go!

Jean S. MacLeod

The Wolf of Heimra (#990)

. . . Fenella knew that in spite of her love for the island,
she had no claim on Heimra yet—until an heir was born.
They were so sure of themselves, these MacKails; they
expected everything to come their way.

Summer Island (#1314)

. . . Cathie's return to Loch Arden was traumatic. She
knew she was clinging to the past, not wanting to let it
go. But change was something you thought of happen-
ing in other places–never in your own beloved glen.

Slave of the Wind (#1339)

. . . Lesley's pleasure at coming home and meeting the
handsome stranger quickly changed to dismay when
she discovered that he was Maxwell Croy—the man
whose family once owned her home. And Maxwell was
determined to get it back again.

HARLEQUIN OMNIBUS

A Jumbo Read!!!

Eleanor Farnes

The Red Cliffs (#975)
... Alison had no particular interest in the old Devonshire cottage she had inherited; her work was in London. But when the overbearing Neil Edgerton wanted to buy it, she was faced with a sudden decision.

The Flight of the Swan (#1280)
... It took six months for Philippa Northern to change her life—to shed her mid-Victorian upbringing, develop her hidden self and find the happiness in living she had never before known. Then a jealous woman threatened to destroy everything!

Sister of the Housemaster (#1335)
... Ingrid hadn't met her sister-in-law's famous brother Patrick and didn't want to. She thought he'd be just as disagreeable as Sylvia. When they did meet, she knew she was wrong, though at first she wouldn't admit it!

Mary Burchell

The Heart Cannot Forget (#1003)
... Deepdene Estate should rightfully be inherited by Antonia's cousin Giles, but for some mysterious reason, he had been cast out. While living there, Antonia slowly uncovers fragments of the mystery, but everything that she learns is directly linked with the woman Giles plans to marry!

Ward of Lucifer (#1165)
... It was a struggle from the start. Norma knew exactly what she wanted, but Justin used her to further his own interests. He found, almost too late, that her happiness meant more to him than his own.

A Home for Joy (#1330)
... After her father's death, Joy accepted the kind offer of a home with her aunt and uncle and cousins. Only later did she discover that the offer was not as kind as it had seemed: there were certain strings attached.

HARLEQUIN OMNIBUS

A Jumbo Read!!!

Susan Barrie

Marry a Stranger (#1034)

. . . If she lived to be a hundred, Stacey knew she'd never be more violently in love than she was at this moment. But Edouard had told her bluntly that he would never fall in love with her!

Rose in the Bud (#1168)

. . . One thing Cathleen learned in Venice: it was very important to be cautious about a man who was a stranger and inhabited a world unfamiliar to her. The more charm he possessed, the more wary she should be!

The Marriage Wheel (#1311)

. . . Admittedly the job was unusual—lady chauffeur to Humphrey Lestrode; and admittedly Humphrey was high-handed and arrogant. Nevertheless Frederica was enjoying her work at Farthing Hall. Then along came her mother and beautiful sister, Rosaleen, to upset everything.

Violet Winspear

Beloved Tyrant (#1032)

. . . Monterey was a beautiful place in which to recuperate. Lyn's job was interesting. Everything, in fact, would have been perfect, Lyn Gilmore thought, if it hadn't been for the hateful Rick Corderas. But he made her feel alive again!

Court of the Veils (#1267)

. . . In the lush plantation on the edge of the Sahara, Roslyn Brant tried very hard to remember her fiancé and her past. But the bitter, disillusioned Duane Hunter refused to believe that she was ever engaged to his cousin, Armand.

Palace of the Peacocks (#1318)

. . . Suddenly the island, this exotic place that so recently had given her sanctuary, seemed an unlucky place rather than a magical one. She must get away from the cold palace and its ghost—and especially from Ryk van Helden.

Harlequin Reader Service

ORDER FORM

MAIL COUPON TO ➤ Harlequin Reader Service,
M.P.O. Box 707,
Niagara Falls, New York 14302.

Canadian SEND Residents TO: ➤ Harlequin Reader Service,
Stratford, Ont. N5A 6W4

Harlequin ◆ Omnibus

OTHER AUTHORS AVAILABLE

Please check volumes requested:

- ☐ Essie Summers 1
- ☐ Jean S. MacLeod
- ☐ Eleanor Farnes
- ☐ Susan Barrie
- ☐ Violet Winspear 1
- ☐ Isobel Chace
- ☐ Joyce Dingwell 1
- ☐ Jane Arbor

- ☐ Anne Weale
- ☐ Essie Summers 2
- ☐ Catherine Airlie
- ☐ Sara Seale
- ☐ Violet Winspear 2
- ☐ Rosalind Brett
- ☐ Kathryn Blair
- ☐ Iris Danbury

- ☐ Amanda Doyle
- ☐ Rose Burghley
- ☐ Elizabeth Hoy
- ☐ Roumelia Lane
- ☐ Margaret Malcolm
- ☐ Joyce Dingwell 2
- ☐ Anne Durham
- ☐ Marjorie Norell

Please send me by return mail the books I have checked.
I am enclosing $1.95 for each book ordered.

Number of books ordered _____ @ $1.95 each = $ _____

Postage and Handling = .25

TOTAL $ _____

Name _____

Address _____

City _____

State/Prov. _____

Zip/Postal Code _____